FINDING LOVE IN ALASKA

MOOSELY

Over You

Copy Editor: Write Girl Editing Services

Cover Design: Alt 19 Creative

Proofreading: FictionEdit.com

Chapter One

LAUREL

There wasn't enough white chocolate mocha in the entire state of Alaska to get Laurel Evans through this already long day, no matter how many shots of espresso were in it. But two grande cups from Black Bear Coffee would have to get her started. They didn't come any larger, and she only had two hands.

Because Charlene was out of stoppers, Laurel was hyper-focused on not spilling her coffees as she pushed the door open with her back. She turned the sharp corner around the coffee shop at Mooseberry Lane and Fourth and screamed. One coffee flew into the air, splattering inches from a massive hoof.

It didn't matter that Laurel had grown up in Sunset Ridge, or that she'd been home for more than six months after a long absence. The unexpected sighting of a bull moose stopped on the street corner, eyeing her curiously from only three feet away, would always threaten an instant heart attack.

She spun on her heel to round the same corner, thankful one coffee remained unscathed. She refused to start off her week being trampled by a startled moose.

Before she could manage a single sip of her precious nectar, however, Laurel plowed into a man and dumped her second mocha all over his blue and white button-up shirt. "I'm so—" She pointed behind her at the antlers poking out from the corner of the building. "Moose. Th-there's a moose." Laurel kept looking over her shoulder, concerned the infamous *Ed* would follow her. But the moose was eagerly licking her first spilled beverage from the pavement. "What do you know? He likes it."

"Laurel."

Her heart stopped at the familiar voice she would never forget. Not if fifty years went by without hearing it. "Chase. Hi."

Since she moved back to Sunset Ridge over

Christmas, she'd done her best to avoid her ex-husband. She was overwhelmed as it was by her family—most especially with her youngest sister who just had a baby. Add in two best friends planning summer weddings a week apart, and facing Chase after the way she left things five years ago was not something her very full plate had room for. If only he wasn't her best friend's brother and included in that same friends' circle, avoiding him would be so much simpler.

"Whoa, look out." Chase pulled her back against him by the shoulder as the local favorite moose shuffled his legs. For a single heartbeat, Laurel surrendered to the protection she'd craved on so many lonely days.

Ed stared straight at them, licking his coffee-splattered lips, then sauntered down Mooseberry Lane toward the bay.

Laurel wriggled free from Chase's hold the second Ed passed the pharmacy and was no longer visible. The urge to sprint to her car was overwhelming, but she wasn't a terrible human being. Plus, she needed more coffee before she decided what item on her list to tackle first. "Hope I didn't burn you. I'm sorry about your shirt."

"I didn't like it much anyway." A half smile tugged at his lips, threatening to lure Laurel into a trap. That tilt of those very kissable lips was what got her into this mess all those years ago. As she fished for napkins in her oversized purse, he asked, "How're Haylee and the baby?"

"Good. They're good." Laurel found three napkins, patting at the largest coffee circle over his shirt pocket. It took seconds to realize her grave mistake. Chase's muscular chest pressed against her fingers was going to get her into an entirely new mess. "Here." She shoved the napkins at him. "I can get more inside—"

"Laurel." His serious tone stopped her midturn toward the entrance. "I really need to talk to you."

She stared off in the direction Ed had ventured but saw no sign of the moose now that she could really use the distraction. For nearly six months, Laurel had been dodging whatever important thing Chase just *had* to tell her. Ever since Ava's New Year's Eve engagement party. "I'm really busy this morning. Maybe another time?"

"You're always busy, Laurel. That's kind of your thing."

Closing her eyes for a beat, she took a deep breath. She was running on barely two hours of broken sleep. Melly, precious angel that she was, had not thought anyone in the house needed sleep. *Silly adults.* Laurel spent half her night buried in spreadsheets and balancing books for her dad's businesses and was now all caught up. But there was a laundry list of things she'd been neglecting: picking out not one, but two bridesmaids dresses, getting a desperately needed manicure, and deciding how to respond to her old boss's email with a generously tempting offer to return to the Florida Keys. None of them held a candle to her desperate need for more caffeine.

"I'll buy you another coffee," Chase offered.

"You sure that's a good idea? You might end up wearing it."

He stepped closer, stopping in front of her. Despite the overwhelming aroma of mocha he now wore, a hint of her favorite cologne drifted to her, tugging her into the past. She pushed away the temptation. Staying grounded in the future was the only way she survived living in this small town with her ex-husband. "I'll take the risk."

As much as Laurel wanted to run the other way, this conversation had been inevitable for months. He'd even given her four additional weeks after Melly came into the world before he brought it up.

Had it not been for Ed just now, she might've squeezed out five. "That moose," she muttered.

"What's that?"

"Coffee first. No bombs dropped until I'm at least halfway through my cup."

"Deal." He held the door and waited for her to reenter Black Bear Coffee.

Behind the register, Charlene wore a knowing smile, promising she'd witnessed both embarrassing incidents. If this was how Monday morning was choosing to behave, Laurel wanted a do-over. For years, these mornings were one of her strengths. She was the rare breed who lived for Mondays. She woke up recharged, ready to face any challenge head-on. Until her sweet niece entered the world. Laurel no longer knew what a normal night of sleep felt like.

Good thing she loved Melly more than she'd ever loved anything else. Even white chocolate mochas.

Arnie Powers adjusted his suspenders at the back of the line as he fixed his attention on Chase's coffee-stained shirt, and smirked. "Hope you didn't get third-degree burns. You should know better than to make this one mad." He cackled, nodding at Laurel.

"You'd think I'd have learned my lesson by now," Chase bantered back, both men allowing Laurel to go in front of them. "I guess I'm addicted to pushing my limits."

"Always thought you two . . ."

Laurel drowned out the conversation happening behind her. Too many locals had opinions about the two of them, and she didn't care to hear which side Arnie was on. It wouldn't change anything. She stared at the two heads in front of her, uncertain whether the line was too long or too short. The sooner she had her coffee, the sooner she'd have to hear whatever it was Chase wanted so badly to tell her. A knot twisting in her stomach warned her she wouldn't like it.

"Heard there was a fire north of town last night," Laurel overheard Arnie say to Chase as she stepped up to the counter and ordered. "Anyone hurt?"

"No, no one was there."

Laurel hated to admit her curiosity was piqued. When she and Chase were first married, he was only a volunteer firefighter working seasonal jobs with demanding hours and solid pay. But when they found out they were pregnant, Chase vowed to find something more stable with benefits and set his sights on one of only two paid positions with the fire department.

After she left town five years ago, she expected

him to abandon that pursuit. She never thought he was passionate about the position that promised more paperwork and politics than fieldwork. She still found it surprising that he was the deputy fire chief, second in charge of the whole fire department.

Maybe I was wrong about what he wanted.

"It was that old shack off Jack Rabbit Creek Road, wasn't it?" Arnie asked. In the brief silence that followed his question, Laurel caught Chase nodding from her peripherals. "Thought the department was going to burn it for practice last summer."

"Everything dried up before we had a chance. Couldn't risk it," Chase answered.

"However it happened, I'm glad that eyesore's gone."

"A lot of people are." Because Laurel knew him, she recognized the evasiveness in his answer. Something bothered him, and she hated even more that it bothered *her*. She'd always care about Chase. That much was inevitable. But this unbreakable thread-thin connection that existed between them should have broken by now.

"Here you go." Charlene held out a fresh coffee to Laurel. "Try not to dump this one out, okay?" Her eyes twinkled as her gaze flickered to Chase, then back to Laurel. "Unless he deserves it, of course. Then, by all means."

"I'm not with him," she said quickly, her cheeks heating. "He was just—"

"You're blushing, sweetie." With a wink, she moved to finish Chase's cup, leaving Laurel to duck her head and pretend to search for stoppers she already knew were on backorder. It was only that Chase Monroe had caught her off guard this morning that she was acting this way. After a solid cup of coffee, distance, and a two-hour nap, she would have her head on straight again.

She took a deep sip, allowing the caffeine to filter through her veins.

"Don't want to take any chances on that one, huh?" Chase's teasing voice forced her eyes open. She stepped out of the way in time to avoid his reaching arm securing napkins. "Me, either."

Laurel checked her phone to avoid the mischievous gleam in his eyes, willing a text or call. Didn't Melly need diapers, or wasn't Cody short a kayak guide? *Of all the mornings for everyone to go radio silent.*

"Let's take a walk." Chase touched her shoulder, urging her toward the door.

"I don't have much time."

He held the door open, obviously seeing right through that lie. "It won't take long."

Laurel eyed her car longingly, but where would she go? The books were caught up. Haylee and her mom were both cranky from a sleepless night, no doubt fighting over the remote. Kinley and Ava were working, as were her brothers. "Fine, but make it quick."

Together they strolled down Main Street toward the water as Laurel sipped on her coffee. Already she wished she'd asked for two. She scanned for Ed, but saw no signs of the moose that had popped up out of nowhere.

"Ed's probably running laps around the town after that sugar rush," Chase offered, causing her to laugh.

A sliver of tension disappeared, allowing Laurel to look ahead and appreciate the bright blue sky that held only a dusting of wispy clouds. The mountaintops welcomed the bright June sun in all their glory. Moments like these made her remember why she loved it here so much. One only had to stare off into the beauty to feel as if even the toughest days were conquerable.

Her happy thoughts were short-lived as the bay approached too quickly. Laurel was less at peace and more desperate to avoid Chase's news every second possible. The knot in her stomach was back with a vengeance. She stalled, checking her phone, willing it to ring. Surely Mom needed her to grab some milk or Dad wanted her to rerun some figures for the store. At this rate, she'd even welcome a call from her middle sister, Sadie. She was *that* desperate.

"What's up with that fire?" she asked. "The one Arnie Powers was asking about."

"Old shack burned down last night. That's all."

Laurel raised an eyebrow at Chase, staring at him through a yawn of his own until he met her eyes. "There's something more. You're worried about something."

They crossed the last street before the water and Chase nodded toward a bench that overlooked the bay. A couple of joggers ran along the sidewalk in front of it before he sat down. "We haven't had enough rainfall this year. That fire could've been a whole lot worse."

"Do you think it was an accident?"

He patted the seat beside him. Laurel went to take another sip of coffee and found her cup empty. Tossing it into a nearby trash bin, she finally relented and joined him. She hardly made contact with the bench before Chase dove right into the heart of the matter. "There's no way to sugarcoat this, so I won't."

The serious tone caused Laurel to stiffen with concern. *Guess we're done discussing the fire.* She hadn't given much thought as to *what* this news was other than *not good*, but now she was afraid it was bad. Too many possibilities raced through her over-active mind, and none of them did anything for that knot in her stomach. "Are you sick? You're not dying, are you?"

"What? No." Chase's light chuckle eased a sliver of her fears. "Nothing like that."

"Then, what?"

"We're still married."

Laurel stared at him, unblinking. "Excuse me?"

"It's a technicality," he explained, his gaze focused on a fishing boat in the bay headed toward deeper waters. "A missed signature."

"We got divorced five *years* ago." Laurel took a deep inhale, willing her brain to function at a higher capacity. Surely there was something she was miss-ing. Something she misunderstood. No one went *five years* believing they were legally divorced only to find out they weren't. "This isn't some movie, Chase. This is real life."

"Jenkins discovered it," he said evasively.

"Six months ago?" She remembered how he'd pulled her into a spare room at Ava's engagement party, insisting he had something important to tell her. Only she asked him to wait until Melly was born before he did. And he'd waited all that time.

He dug his fingers hard into his neck as he rolled it around his shoulders, like he always did when he was avoiding some hard-to-spit-out truth. "More like a year."

"A *year*?" Laurel gripped the bench so hard she thought she might crack a board. "You didn't think to call me?"

"Don't have your new *Florida* number."

Laurel pinned him with narrowed eyes. She hoped he could feel the daggers she was shooting at him. "So, you ask my parents. Or Marc. Or Cody. Or look me up on LinkedIn." Laurel's hands trembled from multiple emotions: irritation, shock, and worst of all, mourning. Sitting still had never been her forte, but now it felt impossible. She sprang to her feet so she could pace, narrowly missing a jogger on the sidewalk.

The day she left Sunset Ridge would be burned into her mind forever. The pain she felt when she shattered the undeniable connection between them and boarded the plane. She left a piece of her soul behind that day, but it was what had to happen. The only fair thing to do in the grand scheme of things.

Why was fate pulling a fast one on her now?

"You get married to someone else while you were away or something?" Though Chase chuckled, she caught the undercurrent in his tone. She wasn't doing this. Not today. Not on such little sleep and not nearly enough coffee.

"How did *you* find out, Chase?"

"I told you. Jenkins."

She bit down on her bottom lip so hard she thought it might bleed. Jenkins had handled the whole divorce. But because Chase paid all the fees, it made irritating sense that the lawyer wouldn't try to contact *her* about the matter. "Whose signature is missing?"

"Yours."

Her TOMS sandals tore up the grass as she marched back and forth, back and forth. The shock of this news made the series of sleepless nights seem pleasant in comparison. How could they have been married this entire time? "Do you have the papers?"

"They're at Jenkins' office."

At least this matter could be put to rest swiftly. "Well, don't just sit there. Let's go." Laurel had to sign them now, before she had too much time to think and lost her nerve. She refused to believe this was fate nudging her at some sappy second chance. They weren't meant to be together, and she couldn't start entertaining that very dangerous thought just because this small detail came to light.

"I thought you were busy," Chase challenged as he followed her to the main sidewalk.

"This is by far the quickest thing I can mark off my to-do list today."

"So, that's it, then?" he said, hurt in his tone that nearly made Laurel's heart crack in two all over again. But she refused to let an ounce of it show in her expression. It was better if he thought she no longer loved him. He deserved the things she couldn't give him.

"This is just a technicality. Nothing more."

He shoved both hands into his pockets, the sun catching the prominent stain on his shirt. She really did feel bad about spilling and eagerly jumped on the chance to change the subject. "I can have that shirt dry-cleaned," she offered a second time. "Or buy you a new one."

"I'll just give it to Zeus. He'll think it's his birthday and rip it to shreds."

"It's a nice shirt," Laurel argued.

Chase let out a laugh. "Not anymore."

"Where is Zeus anyway?"

"At home. I'll pick him up when I run back to change my shirt."

She'd met the lovable Australian shepherd mix once during a birthday cookout at Kinley and Ryder's. Zeus loved playing with their dog, Rowdy. Laurel had tried to ignore him, but the dog had a special affection for her when he wasn't busy chasing his girlfriend or sneaking table scraps. It would do no good to get attached to Chase's dog. But secretly, the dog's interest thrilled her, and she'd discreetly rewarded Zeus with bites of her cheeseburger.

"Do you get to bring him to work often?"

"Yeah, Chief Bauer likes having him around the office." Chase turned his shoulders at her as they walked, wearing that dangerous smile that had stolen her heart in the beginning of their romance. "Tomorrow he gets to come with me to talk to a class-room of kindergarteners."

"He must love that."

"He goes nuts for those kids."

They approached the law office, and Laurel's heart tightened. It shouldn't feel like this a second time, but no matter how hard she pushed down those pesky feelings, some slipped out. It wasn't only the missed signature, but everything those papers represented.

Chase had always wanted a large family, and he was amazing with kids. He didn't need a dog to win them over. They gravitated toward him in droves, like he was the cool uncle of any situation. He deserved to be with someone who could give him what he wanted most.

"Looks like we'll have to wait." Chase tapped a finger against the glass, pointing to the posted sign.

"I can come back after lunch and take care of this."

"After lunch next Monday might do it."

"*Next* Monday?" Panic rose in her chest as she shoved around Chase to read the taped note for herself. She took a deep inhale to keep her exterior self calm. She could kick and scream later, when no one was around to see it.

"It's been five years. One more week going to spoil your plans to take over the world?"

"No, funny guy."

Chase was right. This wasn't the worst thing that could happen. It was only a week, after all. How hard could it be to dodge him for seven measly days? She'd managed almost six months. This week she could hide out in her parents' house and help Haylee with the baby, no matter how much Mom's hovering drove her insane. Work her dad's books remotely. She could order takeout so Ava and Kinley would come to her to discuss wedding plans.

Seven days. Piece of cake.

Chapter Two

CHASE

Chase Monroe lost the fight with a yawn as he rubbed sleep from his eyes. Last night's fire started after he'd fallen asleep on his reclining couch, feet propped up, and Zeus in his lap. He woke to a TV show a couple episodes ahead of where he remembered leaving off. It was well after two in the morning before the crew returned and the station was locked up.

Zeus grumbled at him from beneath the desk as Chase stretched in his rickety office chair, causing it to screech. His neck and shoulders rebelled, but whether from last night or all the hours stuck in this chair, he couldn't be certain.

Despite his exhaustion, he'd tossed and turned last night until his alarm went off. Something about this fire tugged at his instincts, but he couldn't pin what. Chief Bauer was convinced it was a squatter who was long gone after accidentally setting fire to his temporary home. Chase wanted to believe it was that simple. He didn't have time for something more complicated, especially now that the clock was ticking with Laurel. He'd been waiting for the right opportunity to tell her the secret he'd been keeping for months, and thanks to Ed, he finally got his chance this morning.

Another look at the fire site now that the smoke had settled would hopefully put his suspicions to bed and give him time to focus on winning Laurel back. Seven days to convince her the missed signature wasn't merely a coincidence but the very reason they should *stay* married wasn't much time in the grand scheme of things.

He wholeheartedly believed that running into her today had been fate.

If Chase closed his eyes now, he could still smell Laurel's flowery perfume. That sweet scent brought all the old memories to life. He never used to believe in fate, but he had too many encounters these past few years to believe them *all* coincidental—including Ed's timing today. Rather than dismissing the notion, he had learned to lean into the opportunities it granted him.

He knew Jenkins was on vacation when he confessed to Laurel that they were still married. But as set as she already was on ripping up the grass with her incessant pacing, Chase wasn't about to work her up any further by admitting Jenkins and his wife were in Maui, likely sinking their toes in the sand and sipping on Mai Tais. She would've blamed him for telling her today on purpose. Never mind that he couldn't force Ed to do his bidding.

He reached for his coffee cup, not surprised to find it ice cold. He dropped it into the trash bin, not sad to see it go. He rarely drank coffee. Only on the most exhausting days, and even then, he wondered why he suffered through it. If it hadn't been for that late-night fire, he would never have run into Laurel this morning outside of Black Bear. *Or Ed.*

"Maybe everyone around here is onto something by calling that moose a matchmaker, huh, Zeus?" The beast had turned and looked right at them, after all. He hoped to one day tell that story to their grandkids.

Zeus grumbled louder this time, staring up at Chase with large, bored eyes. He wanted to run laps or go fishing or meet new friends at the city park. Being deputy fire chief meant an extraordinary amount of administrative work and more hours behind a computer than he realized was possible. Though he was grateful he could bring Zeus into the station most days, he still felt guilty about the boredom the poor dog must suffer when Chase was hunched over a keyboard for hours.

Saving the budgetary spreadsheet he needed to present at the monthly meeting tomorrow, Chase pushed out of his chair. "You're right. It's about time to meet the chief," he said to Zeus. In half a second, the dog went from sprawled in his bed to popped up on all fours and tail whipping excitedly.

Chase clipped the leash on Zeus' collar, grabbed keys to the station's pickup off his desk, and shouldered the bag with the high-resolution camera and clipboard he'd need to complete the investigation. The sooner he got out there, the sooner he could get back and make his *wife* fall in love with him all over again.

He locked up the office and headed out through the bay.

Halfway to the front door, Chase heard something drop and slide on the concrete floor. Their main fire engine obstructed his view, so he was forced to go around it. Zeus trotted along at his side, perked up at what he must've considered an unexpected adventure.

Chase spotted Marc Evans, Laurel's oldest brother, hugging a clipboard. Hoses, nozzles, and clamps lay neatly on the ground in front of him. Chase watched him for a beat, studying his expression as he inspected the items he was inventorying. He hadn't been out at the fire last night, but the local vet had to be pickier than most volunteers. A sleepless night didn't bode well for a morning surgery.

Before Chase could slip out unnoticed, Zeus whined.

Marc looked up, forcing Chase to wave.

"I'm heading out," he called to Marc.

The two of them had a strained at best relationship since Laurel left Chase. The miscarriage was a secret she begged Chase to keep. She'd been distraught and embarrassed, desperate that no one knew the truth. Even with his own heart cracking in two, Chase never spoke the truth to another soul. With the way Marc scowled at him still, he suspected Laurel never told her family the real reason she left.

Marc, among others, formed their own opinions about why they split. None of those theories painted Chase in a favorable light.

"I'll lock up," Marc called back, focusing his attention on the items laid out before him. "Sorry I didn't make it out last night."

"Nothing to worry about. Plenty did."

Marc nodded, stared at Zeus for a moment, but said no more.

When Laurel and Chase were still together, Marc used to talk to Chase like a friend. Tell him about the surgeries that wore on him the hardest. That was likely why Marc was here now, doing an inventory that wasn't due for another week. It wasn't even Marc's turn on the rotation. Keeping busy at the fire station was his way of blowing off steam after delivering bad news to people about their pets.

"Everything good?" Chase dared to ask, knowing full well it was a crap idea to engage. Zeus tugging at the leash, urging him to the front door, should've cued him in on as much.

"I said I'll lock up when I finish. If anything needs replaced, I'll leave you a note."

Chase only had the energy for so many battles today, so with a nod, he headed for the door.

Zeus barked the second they were outside,

greeting police chief Ryder Grant with enthusiasm on the sidewalk. The dog sniffed Ryder's boots, no doubt detecting his four-legged *girlfriend*, Rowdy. "You headed out to the site?" Ryder asked, scrubbing his hand on the back of Zeus' neck.

"Yeah."

"I'll follow you out."

Zeus hung his head out the window until they hit the city limits and Chase picked up too much speed. Traffic was heavier in the daytime as tourists poured in and out of the only road with access to the seaside town, but soon enough he turned off the highway and onto the dirt road.

Chief Bauer was already on site. Though the investigation was technically in Chase's job description, the chief was walking around the ruins, making his own assessment. He avoided paperwork at all costs, happy to let Chase take care of it. Glenn was better at the media side of things anyway. Chase would happily type up the report if the chief handled the newspaper statement and any other curious reporters.

Zeus strained against his leash, yearning to run free the moment he was out of the truck. But Chase couldn't risk the energetic pup disturbing the scene before he got a good look at everything. Zeus wasn't a trained emergency dog by any stretch of the imagination, but more than once his super-sniffer had found clues Chase might've overlooked on his own.

It was why he brought him today.

"Morning, Chief," Chase called out on approach, his eyes scanning the charred, barren site.

Chief Bauer stood at the center of the blackened earth. A few pieces of scorched wood scattered the rectangular perimeter where the house once stood, along with the black-stained bricks that formed a fireplace and chimney. Branch tips of nearby trees were burned black as well, but thankfully the owner had been driving down the road and caught sight of the fire to call it in before it took out the too-dry surrounding forest.

Only once before had Chase witnessed how quickly a forest fire under the same dry conditions got out of control, burning thousands of acres before it was put out. The same might've happened last night if the initial fire had gone unnoticed.

"I'll let you both take things from here," Glenn said to Chase and Ryder as they met at the edge of the rubble. "I don't suspect you'll find much. Just some squatter whose fire got out of control, and self-calm then he fled like we figured."

Chase nodded, unwilling to say anything before

Glenn drove off and he had a look around for himself now that the smoke had settled. His gut told him this was something more, but unless he could come up with proof, he wasn't going to get anyone worked up.

"I'm announcing a fire ban in town," Glenn called back from his truck, the driver's side door hanging open. "It's drier than we thought."

"Ava won't like the sound of that," Chase mumbled about his sister. She'd been looking forward to a birthday spent around the backyard fire pit he'd helped his soon-to-be brother-in-law Brayden install first thing this spring when the ground thawed. But the way the dry ground was cracked around him, he agreed with Glenn.

"I've kicked more than a couple squatters out of this place in the past year alone," Ryder said about the ruins as Glenn's truck disappeared down the road. "One just a couple of weeks ago. Could be what he thinks."

"Maybe." Chase walked the perimeter, searching for suspicious items—containers that might have been accelerants, clothing, footprints fleeing the scene. But the ground was much too dry for that. No shattered glass lay on the ground to give him any clues, because the windows had either been boarded up or exposed to the elements. The shack hadn't had glass in its windows in years.

Zeus sniffed happily enough, though nothing stopped him in his tracks.

Chase dug his fingers into his neck, pressing them into a knot his office chair had created. "Maybe he's right," he said to Ryder. "A squatter."

"Certainly be easier for you if that was the case," Ryder pointed out. "Not for me, because I have a hefty fine to hand out if we catch the squatter."

He gently kicked at one of the few boards that survived the fire and it turned to ash. "This house was just waiting to go up in flames. Can't believe it took this long, to be honest."

Ryder followed him through the rubble, stopping in front of the only remaining part of the structure still standing: the brick fireplace. "You talk to Henry Davenport yet?" Chase asked as he crouched down to look inside the chimney. A pile of ashes sat there now, but no poker to sift through them with. Though the man owned the property, he didn't live out this way. He and his wife had a place in town. Something about that bothered Chase, but he couldn't pin it.

"He stopped by the station this morning to give his official statement, in case we needed it."

"Anything out of the ordinary about it?"

"You don't think this was a squatter."

"I'm not ruling anything out yet." Chase pushed to his feet and searched around for clues that the fire might've been intentional. It was his job to push at every angle before making a final determination, and that was what he was going to do. Even if the delay aggravated the chief.

"I'll send you a copy of the statement," Ryder offered. "But it's pretty typical. Davenport saw the fire from down the road and called it in. He said he didn't see anyone fleeing the scene, but he was a mile back when he spotted the flames."

Chase went in search of a stick, returning to push around the pile of ashes. The closer he crouched toward the inside of the fireplace, the stronger the sulphury scent hit him. "Do you smell that?" he asked Ryder.

"Kerosene?"

"Yeah." Chase found flakes of paper in the ashes, but no pieces larger than a silver dollar. He'd bag the biggest ones just in case, but he doubted they were anything more than junk mail or flyers. "Looks like whoever it was doused extra paper with too much kerosene and the fire got too hot." He stood, searching once more for clues that this was more than what it seemed. Despite his hope that it was an open-and-shut case so he could focus on a plan to win Laurel back before she inked her signature on those papers, that nagging feeling wouldn't leave him alone. "No one's picked up any hitchhikers headed north?"

"Murph made the call last night while she kept an eye on the scene. Asked the state patrol to keep an eye out. Haven't heard anything yet."

Chase dug out the camera and powered it up.

"You told her yet?" Ryder asked.

Chase had been expecting the question since Ryder drove past Chase and Laurel parting ways outside Jenkins Law Office earlier. The only surprise was that Ryder waited this long to bring it up. Chase felt like a teenage boy with an all-consuming crush, but he wasn't about to let Ryder see that side of him. He'd never hear the end of it. "This morning."

"How'd she take the news?"

"About how I expected."

"And you're not throwing in the towel, even now?"

Chase couldn't hide his goofy, slightly lovestruck grin. "Would you?"

"Geez." Ryder rubbed Zeus' neck when the dog leaned against his leg. "What's your plan, then?"

"I'm working on it." *Seven days*. Why did it have

to feel so final? All the years Laurel was gone and they both believed they were legally divorced, he still held out hope she'd come back to him. He waited, gambling that it was only time she needed to heal and not a whole new life. Now, with that one signature looming over them, it felt absolute. "I just got to keep her out of hiding," Chase mumbled.

"She has grown an affinity for that," Ryder agreed.

Before Chase could ask for any suggestions, the dispatcher's voice echoed on Ryder's shoulder-clipped radio. Chase caught something about shoplifting before Ryder stepped out of earshot.

Chase drew Zeus against his leg and rubbed him hard around the tailbone the way he liked. The dog's tail stood at attention as he grumbled in delight. "What do you think, Zeus? Any ideas, on this fire or Laurel? I'm all ears, buddy."

Zeus barked once, staring up at Chase with a crazy flicker in his eyes. It was the goofy look that won Chase over at the shelter a year ago when they first met. He wanted a big, fluffy dog with personality. Zeus had enough quirkiness for three dogs.

"Got to head back to town," Ryder called, striding toward his patrol car. "Going to Warren's after the meeting?"

"Yeah. Game starts at seven," Chase called back.

After Ryder drove off, Chase took dozens of photos of the scene. Though rain wasn't in the forecast for the next ten days, a heavy gust of wind could alter the evidence. The photos would allow him to review the scene as it was, if needed. Maybe he'd even find something in them that he was overlooking now. "Evidence," he muttered to himself. "Why can't I just accept this for what it is?"

Zeus tilted his head from his spot in the grass nearby, his large ears standing on end, reminding Chase of Yoda.

"You're always good for a laugh, Zeus."

At the sound of his name, the dog popped back to his feet and trotted toward Chase. His leash lay piled on the grass, but as long as they didn't see any critters or end up with curious onlookers, Chase didn't have to worry about him running off.

As Zeus trotted around the perimeter again, Chase bagged the largest shreds of papers from the fireplace. He doubted they'd tell him anything useful, but better to have them than find them missing later.

"All right, boy. Let's go."

Zeus whined, scratching at a board.

"Leave it," Chase ordered, wondering if the dog

detected a faint trace of a rabbit's scent. "It's time to go."

The dog didn't move, just pawed at the ground with more vigor.

Chase's pulse doubled at the prospect of finding something to support his theory of foul play. He moved the board with his boot, the glint of metal catching the sun and nearly blinding him. "A shotgun shell?"

He crouched down before Zeus could get his claws on it and scooped it into an evidence bag. He held it up to exam it better and his excitement dropped. "*Not* a shell casing. Just some lipstick tube." The brass color he thought he'd seen was actually a silver strip. A double heart symbol was etched into the side. Most of the tube was some black leathery substance that hardly seemed marred from the fire. "Lipstick," he muttered in disappointment.

Because he'd already picked it up, he left it bagged.

Chief Bauer would laugh himself to tears at the 'evidence' Chase found. At least they had a better idea that the squatter was a woman. Or maybe two or three squatters ago she was. "Well, this is a bust. Let's go, buddy."

On the drive back to town, he kept thinking

about the tube of lipstick. Laurel was wearing a light pink shade this morning; she'd left the evidence on her coffee cup. If he remembered right, she had some of that same shade of lipstick in one of those boxes at his place. She used to leave it on his shirt collar, and the memory made him smile.

Laurel had fled so quickly after the miscarriage that she only took a couple of suitcases' worth of belongings with her. The rest of her things, she'd left behind for him to deal with. He boxed most of them up, expecting her to send for them or even ask him to drop them off at her parents' house. But she never did. A dozen boxes or more sat stacked in a spare bedroom's closet.

Pulling into the station, Chase felt more than a glimmer of hope. He felt renewed determination. "Zeus, I have an idea how to win her back." He scrubbed his hand over the dog's neck, winning a hearty lick to the cheek. "Yes, you can help."

Chapter Three

LAUREL

"If anyone wakes Melly up, I'll douse you in sugar water and feed you to the mosquitoes myself," Haylee Evans threatened Laurel and their mom, her droopy-lidded eyes narrow and fierce. For the first time in over three hours, the house was completely silent, and no one was brave enough to turn on a muted TV.

"I'll help you," Laurel volunteered, fighting another yawn. What were days without massive tear-inducing yawns? She didn't know anymore.

"If you'd just stop picking her up every time she cries—"

Haylee held up a hand like a stop sign. "Mom, *don't* go there right now." Sweet Haylee, the youngest of the five Evans siblings, looked scarier than the black bear Laurel discovered digging through their trash a few weeks back. But no one in this house was particularly peachy without a semi-normal amount of sleep. Except Cody. He could survive on no sleep for weeks and still be as chipper as the morning sun. She supposed if she was able to winter in exotic places like New Zealand and Barbados, she'd be unstoppably happy all the time, too.

"Haylee, I'm just trying—"

"Mom, not now!"

"Who wants some chips and salsa?" Laurel offered, falling right back into her role of referee slash peacekeeper as she did every time Haylee and Mom were about to go at it. It was the reason Laurel moved back to Sunset Ridge.

She was the first one Haylee, nineteen and away at her first year in college at the time, told about being pregnant. Haylee was terrified how furious her parents would be, especially when they discovered the father was not going to be in the picture at all. Laurel still had nightmares about that phone call. Haylee sobbing hysterically into the phone, terrified of the future. Tears silently streaming down Laurel's face on the other end as she took charge and reassured Haylee she was going to be there by her side the whole time. It had been shockingly easy to give up her successful luxury real estate career in the Florida Keys.

Haylee swiped a chip before Laurel was able to set the bowl on the island counter. "Did you get the *good* salsa this time?"

"Stop being a brat, or I'll make sure you get the extra spicy kind," Laurel teased.

Cautiously, Haylee dipped a dinky corner of her chip in the salsa bowl and tested it for herself. "Idle threats," she muttered to Laurel, sticking out her tongue. For a blink, they were kids again—Laurel a teenager and Haylee an innocent seven-year-old. Another blink, and reality returned.

"Did either of you get the laundry switched over?" Mom asked both girls as she helped herself to a chip without salsa. "Melly has a lot of onesies in there."

Haylee looked on the verge of tears at another chore, so Laurel jumped in as she had so many times before. "I'll do it now." Never mind that Melly had more clothes than any baby could possibly need, and most of them were clean. *Peacekeeper. That's your role.*

Hovering at the top of the carpeted basement steps, she turned back to say, "Ava and Kinley are coming over soon. We'll stay in the basement, out of everyone's way. But watch for them so they don't forget and ring the doorbell."

"Wedding planning?" Mom guessed.

"Yeah. They want to make sure they don't pick out all the same things." Laurel shook her head at that. She'd opted for a simple wedding. One that didn't require a heap of planning or too many minute decisions. *Not that it matters now.* Laurel had mastered compartmentalizing, and she could tuck her pesky emotions away. She was determined to be a good co-maid of honor—for both of her best friends.

"You're going to bail on me," Haylee mumbled. "It's cool."

"It's only for the evening." Watching Haylee yawn hard enough to draw moisture at the corners of her eyes, Laurel relented. "I'll take the midnight-to-five shift tonight. That way you can get some real sleep."

"Really?" Haylee did cry then. Happy tears, judging by her relieved expression.

"Have you run that by your father?" Mom chimed in, not nearly as big a fan of Laurel's flexible work hours as Dad seemed to be. Mom retired from nursing two weeks before Haylee dropped the bomb about the baby on her parents and still hadn't figured out how to take it easy—or let anyone else, for that matter.

"It'll be fine," Laurel reassured Mom. She almost volunteered for more overnight Melly shifts that would give her an excuse to avoid Chase until Jenkins was back in town. But Ava would kill her if she missed the birthday cookout, no matter what her excuse. The two had spent enough years not talking, and Laurel wasn't about to jeopardize their recently renewed friendship. Looking at Haylee, she added, "Only if you tell Dad I'm taking tomorrow off."

"Happily," Haylee announced, swiping at the fresh tears.

Laurel hurried downstairs, pulled the baby clothes out of the dryer, and moved the wet load of towels. Then she set to folding Melly's many, many outfits.

She'd been a trooper through this whole pregnancy thing with Haylee, shoving down her own emotions to focus on caring for her sister and niece.

But moments like these, she closed the door and let tears stream silently down her cheeks, mourning the loss of a child she never got to meet. She swiped at the moisture covering her cheeks, wondering how different her life would be if their child had come into the world. One her family never knew she lost.

She and Chase would still be happily married. Maybe they'd have two kids by now. A third on the way. *Not possible anymore.*

Laurel sniffled as she sobbed harder.

Five years ago, running away without an explanation seemed the easiest answer to everything. She always meant to tell her family *why* she left. But the more time that went by, the harder that confession became until she decided against it completely. *No need to dredge up the past.*

She cried until the tears dried up, then shoved her emotions back down into the imaginary box she kept under lock and key. Her best friends would be here soon, and she didn't want them to wonder why she was upset. Or worse, Mom to pop in unexpectedly and question her puffy cheeks.

Laurel let out a laugh, wondering how her family would take the news that she and Chase were still legally married.

Of course she wouldn't tell them that. No point when it would all be finalized in a week.

It doesn't have to be.

The quick thought startled Laurel and she dropped the purple onesie with the baby elephant. It lodged in the narrow opening between the dryer and the wall, forcing Laurel to stretch her arm longer than it wanted to go.

"Don't be ridiculous," she muttered. "There is no future there."

Laurel folded the last onesie, dropped it on the top of the folded pile in the laundry basket, and checked her face in the wall mirror beside the door. The redness in her cheek was nearly gone, so she pasted on her smile and returned upstairs.

The house was blissfully quiet. *Melly's still asleep.* If Mom and Haylee were bickering, they were doing it with whispers.

"Momma's asleep," Mom said when Laurel topped the steps, nodding at Haylee whose head rested on her folded arms in front of the half-empty chip bowl, her sleeve covered in salsa. If Laurel wasn't mistaken, a chunk of tomato was stuck in her hair. "I'm not *that* brave," Mom said with a soft laugh, leaning back against the counter.

Laurel set the folded basket on the passthrough window counter. "How did you handle *five* of us?"

"I think I blacked out the worst of it."

"You mean the Sadie years?"

"Oh yes, those most especially." Sadie Evans was the middle sister, second youngest, and the most rebellious in nature of them all. She made the rest of them look like angels, and Laurel knew that was saying something. Her sister currently lived in Anchorage and still had not come home to meet her niece. The only one in the family who stood a chance at convincing her to was Cody, but no one had asked that favor of him yet. Life was chaotic enough without Sadie amplifying the storm.

That moment felt like the one to tell Mom about losing her baby. *Tell her, Laurel. She'll understand.* But she hesitated too long, and just as the words were about to form, Ava and Kinley knocked quietly on the kitchen door and waved.

Haylee didn't stir. Now that she was out cold, only Melly could wake her.

"You have good friends," Mom said about their quiet arrival. "But if they get too excited about cake or whatever and wake Melly, I can't save you from your sister."

Laurel patted Mom on the shoulder in passing.

"I'd stand a better chance stealing a grizzly bear's salmon dinner."

Grabbing sodas and a pre-prepared plate of cheese, caribou summer sausage, and crackers, Laurel led her two best friends through the kitchen and down into the basement. No one dared whisper a thing until they were in the family room, as far from Melly's afternoon napping spot as they could get. Still, Laurel shut the door to be safe.

"Your parents basically live in a log mansion," Kinley said when Laurel leaned against the door and let out a heavy exhale. "Melly have superhuman hearing or something?"

"Yes."

"You look like you haven't slept in a week," Ava said, setting an overflowing pastel blue—her prominent wedding color—binder on the coffee table. Ava had always been the meticulous planner, but this was excessive even for her.

"Try four." Laurel nodded at the binder as she passed out sodas. "Are we planning your wedding or buying an island and opening a resort? I bet you even have a treasure map in that thing."

"If I see something I like, I print it and it goes in the binder," Ava admitted with a sheepish smile.

Kinley aimed the remote at the TV and turned

on a reality wedding show about multiple brides attending each other's weddings and rating them. "Neither of you are allowed to bring scorecards to each other's weddings," Laurel said, only half teasing. It was bad enough that the two were getting married one week apart. Was she the only one who saw the drama that would cause?

"But it would be fun—"

"Nope." Laurel cut Kinley off before the idea could take root. "As co-maid of honor for *both* of you, I forbid it."

"Do you think the guys would kill me if I made them wear pink ties?" Kinley asked, her attention fixed on her phone screen. Instead of a binder, she had her ideas saved on a Pinterest board.

Laurel sputtered a laugh, imagining Chase's reaction when forced to wear pink. She could picture the sour expression on his scrunched-up face when she tried to put it on him.

"Laurel?"

"What now?"

"What do you think about this for a centerpiece?" Ava unclipped a page from her binder and held it out. "Is it too extravagant? I can make these myself, but—"

"It's your wedding. What do *you* want?"

"I want the guys wearing pink ties," Kinley chimed in, a mischievous twinkle dancing in her eyes. "Ryder didn't want to make any *girly* decisions, so pink ties it is."

For over an hour, Laurel scanned over hundreds of pictures for both weddings. She was good at multi-tasking, and keeping the two very different concepts separate became easier with each passing minute. Laurel lost herself in the excitement of wedding plans. These two were her very best friends, after all. For the first time in weeks, she again felt like the successful businesswoman she was.

"I could order a pizza," she offered.

"Hawaiian!" Kinley suggested. She'd given up on her wedding Pinterest board and switched over to the honeymoon one twenty minutes ago, and it showed.

"Who puts pineapple on—"

Melly's cries tore through the house like a tornado siren, silencing the girls. They stared at the door, then at each other.

"On second thought, maybe we could head to Warren's instead. I've been dying to try his smoked salmon pizza," Laurel suggested. Any ounce of guilt she felt at abandoning her sister was eliminated by her promise to take the overnight shift.

"You two go," Ava said, closing her binder and standing. "I need to stop by the store and help Lydia close. It's her first time." Ava owned the Forget Me Not Boutique. When she wasn't busy with wedding plans or spending time with her fiancé, Brayden, and their dog, Elsie, she was working.

"We can bring the pizza to you," Kinley offered.

Ava waved away the suggestion. "Seafood on pizza isn't really my thing." Hugging her binder to her chest, she sternly looked at both Kinley and Laurel. "Friday at six. Don't be late."

"We'll be there," Laurel promised. In the past six months, she'd learned to appreciate how valuable deep, meaningful friendships were. She never wanted to fight with Ava again. Not when they'd finally gotten past Laurel splitting on Ava's brother. Even if Chase would be there too, she'd never miss Ava's birthday cookout.

It wasn't until they were seated at the bar at Warren's Sea Shack and the pizza order was in that Laurel heard his laugh. Chase had an infectiously sexy laugh that always made her tingly inside. She could pick it out of a chorus of laughter.

A pack of men filed in through the entrance, headed straight for the largest table near the biggest two flat-screen TVs in the restaurant.

"Baseball game," Kinley said seconds before Ryder came up behind her and circled his arms around her. Laurel pushed the straw around her soda, wishing she'd ordered a margarita instead as she pretended to ignore the sickeningly sweet display of affection happening beside her. *Why did I volunteer for the overnight shift again?*

"Laurel, hey."

She stared at her cup, afraid to look up. "Hi."

"Didn't think you liked baseball." Chase leaned an elbow on the bar counter, forcing Laurel to glance at him. He shouldn't smell that good. Or look that good in just a black polo with the Sunset Ridge Fire Department logo stitched above the left breast pocket.

"I don't. Just here for the pizza."

"On Taco Tuesday?"

How many Tuesdays had they come here together while they were dating, and even after they were married? Laurel pushed away the memories before the emotions could seep in. "I wanted pizza."

As if on cue, Warren carried over their smoked salmon pizza on a wooden tray, propping it on a stand. "Here you ladies go. Careful, it's hot." Warren nodded at Chase and Ryder, taking quick drink orders.

Laurel plated herself a steamy hot slice, hoping Chase would take the hint and go sit at the table with the rest of the volunteer fire department. It was already the bottom of the first. Very little kept him from him from watching the Rockies play.

"Hey, if you have some time this week, you still have a few things at the house. Mind going through them?"

"You've waited five years," Laurel said, her tone icier than she intended. "What's a few more weeks?"

"I'm remodeling. Knocking out the closet they're in." When Laurel took a bite of pizza instead of responding, he added, "They're in the way. I'd drop them off at your parents' place, but there's stuff in there you might not want your mom to see."

A knot formed at the base of Laurel's throat. *Baby stuff.* That's what he meant. A sliver of gratitude shot through her that he didn't say it out loud. Kinley didn't know. No one but the two of them and her brother Cody knew about the miscarriage. Chase had kept his word.

"I'm free tomorrow," Chase added.

"I can't tomorrow." Laurel didn't have a good reason, especially with the unexpected day off. Even though she would sleep in, Laurel never slept later than eight even when she tried. "Promised Cody I'd help him out. We'll figure out a time." When Chase didn't immediately follow Ryder to their table, she added, "Soon. This week. Happy?"

Chase set his phone on the counter. "I need your number."

"No, you don't."

"I need to know when you're swinging by so I can be there to let you in."

Chase not having her number—and more importantly, her not having his—was the only barrier she had between them. She didn't need the temptation to text him in the middle of the night when she couldn't sleep. When she left Sunset Ridge, she made a promise to herself to let Chase move on so he could find someone better.

If she had his number, that promise would be a whole lot harder to keep.

"Laurel, it's just a phone number."

Because Kinley and half the volunteer fire department, including Marc, were staring at them, Laurel typed in her number. Anything to make him go away before they had another reason to talk about them. As she entered the digits, she could feel her oldest brother's disdain on the other side of the restaurant.

"Here." Laurel shoved the phone back at Chase's chest. "Go watch your game. Your team already scored a run, and the bases are loaded."

"I knew it," Chase said, leaving her with a wink.

"What is *that* about?" Kinley asked in a low tone.

"Nothing important."

Kinley whapped her shoulder with the back of her hand. "Secrets don't make friends. You should know that better than anyone."

If only Kinley knew how spot-on she was.

"Promise not to say a word?" Laurel asked through gritted teeth, her slice of delicious pizza growing colder with each passing second. "I mean it, Kin. Not a word."

"Fine. I promise."

"We're still married."

"What?" Kinley's exclamation turned heads—all of them. Everyone in the restaurant stared at the two women at the bar, Chase and Marc included.

Laurel sucked in a deep exhale. "Nice discretion."

"I'm sorry," Kinley apologized, lowering her tone to ask, "It's just, *how* is that possible?"

"I missed a signature on the papers, I guess."

Kinley dished another slice of smoked salmon pizza onto her plate. "And it took five years for someone to catch that? Does that actually happen these days? I feel like this is a movie or something."

"No," Laurel said immediately. "Not a movie. Maybe *The Twilight Zone*," she added the second in a mumble as she reached for her soda.

"Does Chase know?"

Laurel's gaze drifted to her ex-husband, who was clapping in excitement as his team scored another run. At this rate, the Rockies would run away with the lead. She rarely watched baseball, but when she did, she liked the game to be more even. One team scoring all the runs was boring to watch. "Who do you think told me?"

"What about Ava? Does she know?"

Laurel cringed at that. She didn't want to tell her, but she wanted the repercussions of keeping that secret even less. They were all getting along again, like they used to in high school. A tight-knit trio. Now was not the time to ruin it with more secrets. "I'll tell her," she promised. "It's not my fault she ditched us for work tonight."

"What did Chase want with your number?" Kinley pressed.

"Can we not talk about my *ex* anymore?" Laurel flashed her a purposefully cheesy smile, turning so her back completely blocked Chase from her view. "I thought we were wedding planning. Tell me more about these pink ties."

Chapter Four

CHASE

The Rockies had the game won by the third inning, but Chase didn't use that excuse to leave Warren's when he noticed Laurel and Kinley pay their check and slip away. He'd hoped they'd come join the table, but instead Kinley gave Ryder a small wave as Laurel hurried out the door.

With Marc Evans sending intermittent threatening glares from across the table, Chase didn't dare try to coax them to stay.

"I'm out," Ryder said to Chase, pushing out of his chair when the Rockies took the field in victory, much to the dismay of all the Royals fans at the table. "You ready?"

"Yeah." Some of the guys would stay until close to watch sports updates their wives wouldn't tolerate at home, but Chase had a renovation project to get started on if he wanted his excuse to Laurel to be believable. He could build retaining walls in his sleep, but he knew very little about knocking down closet walls. So far, he hadn't even moved the boxes out of the closet he planned to demolish.

Chase paid and headed toward the door to wait for Ryder. They'd left their trucks at the fire station after the monthly meeting concluded, as had most of the guys, and would need to walk back. Weaving through mostly empty tables, he spotted Henry Davenport and his wife Crissy enjoying a late lobster dinner. Warren's most expensive meal on the menu.

"Celebrating an anniversary tonight?" Chase asked, stopping at their table.

"My birthday's next week," Crissy answered, dabbing her lips with a cloth napkin and staining it with a dark shade of pink lipstick. Warren's Sea Shack was both the main bar and the only fine-dining establishment in town on Tuesday nights. "Dragged Henry out early so he didn't have to worry about forgetting. He's been extra forgetful lately."

The urge to ask Henry a few questions about the fire tugged at Chase, but when Ryder came up behind him, stopping at the table, he decided to leave well enough alone. The statement Henry gave was generic. *Too generic.* Chase felt it was missing something, but couldn't pin *what*. Yet, a celebratory dinner was not the time to question it.

"Birthday lobster," Henry said to Ryder with a helpless shrug and a crooked smile.

"Warren makes the best," Ryder added, eyeing the door. No doubt eager to spend some time with Kinley before the night was completely over. Maybe even a subtle hint for Chase to leave well enough alone about what everyone considered an open-and-shut investigation. If Ryder didn't have any suspicions, why should Chase?

Chase was about to wish them a good evening when he saw Crissy kick Henry's boot.

"Say, Chase, did you happen to finish that report on the fire?" Henry asked.

"It'll be done soon," Chase answered. "Just have a few things to finalize before I sign off on it."

"No rush. Was just curious to read it. See if you found any clues about the culprit, though I suspect whoever it was is long gone. Can't imagine anyone who set a fire—even on accident—and then ran, would be stupid enough to hang around town." Henry reached for his beer, but didn't get the cup to his lips before he asked, "State patrol find any hitchhikers headed north?"

"Not that I've heard," Ryder answered.

"Doubt they will," Crissy muttered. "No one wants to pay *that* fine."

Starting a fire and leaving the scene could cost the culprit up to twice the amount of fighting the fire in the state of Alaska. Millions of dollars in some cases where thousands of acres burned as a result. But panic could cause people to act irrationally and flee, hoping never to be caught rather than be a decent citizen.

"Good thing we got the fire out before it became a real issue," Ryder added. "You folks have a good night."

Outside, Chase didn't have the chance to ask Ryder about the fire because his buddy beat him to the line of questioning on a different matter entirely.

"So, you've got a plan. With Laurel."

"A poor one." He didn't know what he hoped to accomplish with Laurel coming over and going through boxes of her things. The baby boxes would be hard for both of them. He wondered if she even missed some of her old clothes. Maybe he hoped that buried in those boxes somewhere were good memories. Ones that would remind her why they fell in love in the first place.

It was a long shot at best, but currently the only one Chase had.

Ryder shoved his hands in his pockets as a chilly summer breeze rose off the water. "I can't wait to hear this one."

"Know anything about home renovations?"

"You're kidding."

"Going to knock out a closet."

"And then what?"

Chase shrugged. "Haven't gotten that far yet. Guess I could make a new master suite. Or a bigger closet." The room in question wasn't being used for anything other than storage. His dreams of filling the five-bedroom house with a bunch of kids seemed further away every day. Chase tried to move on in the earlier years after Laurel left, but no one had held a candle. He couldn't imagine starting and growing a family with anyone else. She was it. The One. Never mind that her family didn't care for him anymore. Or that Laurel was better at avoiding him than anything else.

The two stood on the sidewalk outside the fire hall in front of their respective trucks. Ryder was laughing at him, and Chase didn't blame him. "Big romantic gestures were never her thing," Chase added in defense.

"Just be careful not to give *her* the sledgehammer. I don't want to arrest either one of you this week." Ryder clapped him on the shoulder. "Kinley's waiting."

Chase got into his truck so he wasn't left standing alone on the sidewalk. Just because downtown *looked* deserted didn't mean it was. Plus, Zeus would no doubt be up from his nap. The pup had overexerted himself with a classroom of kindergarteners earlier that afternoon, but his batteries recharged quickly. He'd need to stretch his legs before they could cuddle up on the couch and figure out where they left off on their TV show.

He drove east, away from the bay, turning onto a residential street. Though Sunset Ridge never got completely dark this time of year, it was dusky enough for his headlights to automatically kick on. They lit up someone walking a block ahead.

It took him only half a second to recognize her silhouette.

Laurel.

She'd left Warren's two hours ago. He expected her to go back to her parents' house or maybe be with Kinley. Why was she walking alone on this side of town? Chills danced up his spine, reminding him there could be danger. More than the unknown tourists in town, there might be a possible arsonist.

Sure, it was a stretch. But he wasn't going to gamble with Laurel's life.

Slowing as he reached her, he rolled down the passenger window. "Need a ride?" he called, coming to a stop in the middle of Blueberry Lane.

"No, I'm good."

"Where you headed?" She was walking in the opposite direction of her parents' house, almost as far from it as she could get without leaving the city limits.

"Just out for a walk. Is that a crime?"

"It's late. Might not be safe."

Laurel gave him a stern *are you kidding me?* look. "This isn't some crime-ridden city, Chase. Don't try to tell me there might be some serial killer on the loose either, because I won't buy it. You'd think I've never gone for walks in worse places."

"Please, let me give you a ride."

Several beats of tense silence followed.

"Laurel?"

She let out a huff of air. "Fine," she relented, much to Chase's surprise. "But I'm not ready to go home yet. I still have two hours and twenty-one minutes before I'm on Melly duty. I'm not wasting them." She hopped in the truck and pointed her finger at him. "No talking. I want silence. Hence, the walk, *alone*."

Chase lifted his hands in surrender as she fastened her seat belt. "I have to stop at home and get Zeus," he said, smirking when he felt her narrowed eyes burn into him. But he was moving too quickly down the road for her to bail now. "Then we'll go for a *quiet* drive."

"Fine."

Laurel waited in the truck while Chase ran inside and got Zeus. After a quick stretch of his legs in the fenced backyard, the dog eagerly followed Chase to the truck and darted into the back seat like a rocket. He hopped onto the center console before Chase climbed behind the wheel, catching Laurel giggling at the overzealous greeting.

"He's used to sitting up front," Chase said in mild apology.

"He can still sit up here," Laurel said to the dog,

gathering him into her lap, not a bit bothered by his fifty pounds. "You won't talk my ear off, will you, bud? I might even steal you tonight. How do you feel about fussy babies?"

Chase pulled out of the driveway, biting back the urge to tell her about Zeus' last encounter with an infant. The way he eagerly licked every inch of the little girl who screamed at first but ended up in a fit of giggles within seconds. He'd make the perfect family dog. But since Laurel had asked for quiet, he wasn't going to risk her cutting their unexpected time together short.

"Where're we going?" she asked Chase when he turned onto the main road along the bay and headed out of town.

He answered with a devious smile.

"I'm not going on any moonlit walks or anything," she added. "Not that there's much moon-light this time of year. But you know what I mean." Laurel stroked Zeus' neck, and much to his surprise, the normally restless dog settled in her lap. Chase had never seen him *not* demand to stick his head out the window. Or at least nose up the glass from the inside. It was uncanny how instantly calm he was around her.

Chase turned off the highway onto Jack Rabbit

Creek Road without a word, but Laurel seemed to put the pieces together without him cluing her in.

"Why are we out here?" she asked. "Are you worried someone will start another fire or something? It looks like the old shack is gone. Except for that creepy fireplace."

Parking along the dirt road, Chase turned in his seat toward Laurel. "For someone who demanded silence, you're sure talking a lot." Before she could do more than drop her mouth, he added, "Put him on the leash if you two come out."

He didn't take his camera or anything more than a nearly dead cell phone. Chase wasn't sure what he hoped to find at the site of the recent fire. He highly doubted the culprit would return to assess the damage. But running into the owner had Chase's thoughts stirred up once again. Chief Bauer wasn't happy with Chase's decision to delay the report another day, but something tugged at him.

He heard the truck door close and the rattle of Zeus' tags as the pup shook his whole body in excitement.

"You really like this job?" Laurel asked, her tone curious as the pair approached him. "Deputy fire chief?"

"Most days," Chase answered without looking back at her. He could sense her presence as strongly now as he could years ago. It was impossible for them to both be in a crowded room, even in opposite corners, without that awareness raising the hairs on his arms. No one else had ever had that effect on him. "I could do without all the spreadsheets and hours spent behind a computer."

Laurel let out a soft laugh that transported him back to a time when conversations like this were normal. Her laughter was a regular part of his day, one he looked forward to almost as much as he did kissing her. "I always thought you'd go back to being a deckhand. You liked having large chunks of time off."

"Nah, that life is behind me now." Chase approached the fireplace, shining his cell phone flashlight into the dark cavern and ensuring he wouldn't startle any wildlife. He crouched down once again, using the stick he'd procured the last time to poke around the ashes.

"What are you looking for?"

"Good question." He wanted to share his theory with Laurel, but he didn't need yet another person telling him he was making too much out of nothing.

The evidence supported the main theory, and he could find nothing to shed any doubt on it.

"You don't think the fire was an accident." Not an ounce of question in her voice, only conclusion.

"It's a gut feeling."

"You're never wrong about those."

Chase felt a soft glow of warmth in his chest from her words. "Rarely."

"What do you think this *person* was trying to accomplish by burning down an old shack no one's lived in for what? Ten, fifteen years?"

A rustle in the trees drew their attention away from the fireplace. Chase popped to his feet, protectively stepping in front of Laurel. The gun he rarely used was in the truck, too far away to protect them should they need it. Through the dusk, two eyes reflected the half moon.

"It's a moose," Laurel whispered.

The outline of the beast became clearer the longer Chase stared at it. "Probably Ed."

"There *is* more than one moose in the world, you know," Laurel argued, squinting at the animal hesitating at the tree line. Zeus let out a soft whine, and the moose scuffled backward, running away.

"That wasn't Ed," Chase said.

"See!" Laurel turned toward him. "Wait, what?"

"No antlers. That was a cow."

"A girl moose." Laurel let out a soft laugh that quickly grew heartier. "That's what the local celebrity moose needs. A girlfriend."

"Well, if she's destined for that fate, it'll be a few months. Rutting season isn't until the fall." Chase enjoyed the twinkle in Laurel's eyes and stared long enough that she looked away. "Maybe she's just staking her claim now before all the other girl moose descend on Sunset Ridge."

"You're ridiculous."

Zeus barked, as if in agreement.

"Traitor."

Laurel dug her phone out of her back pocket and flipped on the light to help cut through the dusky shadows. "What are we looking for?" she asked Chase. "I want to help."

"You believe me."

"Like I said, I know your gut feelings."

"I've already studied the fire patterns and burn marks. They're consistent with the fire originating in the fireplace and spilling out. The only thing we might find is something I missed hiding in the rubble. A clue."

"Clues. Got it."

For over an hour they searched through the ashes

and charred pieces of boards. Most of them disintegrated with hardly a bump. Chase scoured the site with twice the determination he had yesterday, fueled by Laurel's belief in him. The same belief that had convinced him to pursue the deputy fire chief position, despite his lack of experience. He beat out three other more qualified candidates because of it.

"I have to get home," Laurel said to him, switching off the light on her phone. His had died ten minutes ago, when he'd been forced to use the faint moonlight instead. They should've left when his phone shut off in case there was an emergency and someone needed to get hold of him. But he'd been so determined to find a *real* clue. Anything to convince him to hold off on signing that investigation report tomorrow afternoon.

He dug his fingers into his neck. "Okay, let's get you home."

"I'm sorry we didn't find anything." Laurel sounded as though she meant it, and that tugged a sad smile across his lips.

After wiping Zeus' paws with an old towel to get the soot off, they loaded up in the truck and headed back into town. The dog still preferred to ride in Laurel's lap, curled into a ball and falling asleep as soon as they hit the highway.

"Thanks," Laurel said when he pulled into her parents' driveway. The massive log cabin was one of the largest homes in town, second only to the Sunset Ridge Lodge. Once upon a time he was a welcome guest inside those walls, especially for Sunday family dinners.

"For what?"

"You know what." She hesitated long enough that he thought he might lean over the center console, draw her to him with his fingers hooked under her chin, and kiss her. Remind her why they were still meant to be together. If that missed signature wasn't fate sending them a sign, he didn't know what was.

But Laurel slid Zeus carefully out of her lap and slipped out of the truck before he could so much as reach a hand forward. "Don't forget about those boxes," he said to her.

"Good night." With that, she closed the door and trekked up the rest of the vehicle-cluttered driveway. Last he knew three of the Evans siblings, plus Melly now, lived with Jerry and Beth. Only Marc had his own place. And then there was Sadie, only she was in Anchorage last he heard. There was less drama when Sadie wasn't around, but at the moment it was a fairly full house.

He waited with headlights dimmed until Laurel waved to him at the door and slipped inside. "Zeus, if you have any bright ideas, now's the time to share them." The dog looked up at him with wide eyes, as if to say he was already doing his part.

Chapter Five

Laurel

Second coffee of the late morning in hand, Laurel headed down the block toward Evans Kayaking Adventures and Rentals. That there was no closer parking was a good sign. One that matched the books she'd combed over this morning while she fed Melly a bottle in the twilight hours.

Cody managed the seasonal family side business without much interference from Dad. That was the best thing about their father. He was willing to back their dreams financially and let them spread their wings with very little micromanaging on his part. As long as things stayed in the black, Dad was content enough to manage the family-owned downtown store, Evans Outfitters.

"Didn't expect to see you out of bed before noon," Cody teased her when the door to the beach-themed kayaking shop closed behind her. With the large shells and white-painted driftwood signs adorning the light blue walls, Laurel always thought the shop was better suited for somewhere like North Carolina. But it was Mom's design, and Cody wouldn't risk hurting her feelings by redecorating in a masculine theme.

"Melly hardly cried last night, thanks to me. You're welcome."

"I can sleep through anything, Melly included." Cody flashed her that charming smile that made half the girls in town swoon on sight. With his hazel-blue eyes and shaggy blond hair just long enough to have a wave to it, that smile only made him *more* dangerous.

"I know. It's not fair that you're the only Evans blessed with that gift." She leaned on the counter with folded arms as Cody typed something into the computer. "Business seems to be pretty good today. Didn't see a lot of kayaks left."

"It's tourist season," Cody said, as if that were the only explanation needed.

"Right." She fiddled with a cup holder full of Evans Outfitters pens. Cody rented kayaks and even sent groups off on guided tours that required a boat to haul them out to a glacier-fed lake. But any of the gear or clothing they might need, Dad sold at the store two blocks away. It was a clever business arrangement that benefited both places.

"Did you need something? Maybe want to take a kayak out?" Cody asked without taking his eyes off the screen.

Laurel *had* dressed in activewear, though it was subconscious when she did so. Except the water-proof jacket tied around her waist now. She grabbed that with intent on the way out the door. "Advice?" she finally said in answer, her voice quiet despite how no one else was around. The guides were out with tourist groups, leaving Cody to man the shop alone.

He held up his finger as he finished entering something into the computer. Once finished, he turned his full attention to her. "Yes, dear sister?" She loved that most about him. How Cody would put down anything he was doing to really listen. That superpower was probably the reason he had a good relationship with Sadie while the rest of them didn't.

"Two things."

"Shoot."

"Sadie still hasn't come to meet Melly. She's a month old come Sunday."

Cody nodded thoughtfully, then said, "I'll talk to her."

"Thanks." She took a swig of coffee, because the next thing wasn't so easy to put into words. In fact, she wondered if bringing it up was a mistake. She trusted Cody more than anyone, but that wasn't why she hesitated. It was because he gave advice she *needed* to hear, even if she didn't like it. Good advice. Solid. Insightful. Thought-provoking.

"You won't be happy with yourself if you leave here and don't spit it out."

Laurel sighed dramatically, because her little brother was right. "I'm still legally married to Chase."

"Huh."

She stared at him as if he'd grown a second head. "That's your reaction?"

"It's not that surprising, that's all."

"Sure shocked me. We were divorced for five years, or so we both thought until Jenkins found a missing signature." Laurel still wasn't certain how it was possible for that to slip through the cracks for so long. Before Cody could ask about that signature, she added, "Jenkins won't be back in town until Monday. Apparently, he's in Hawaii. I have to wait until he gets back to sign it."

Cody's gaze flickered to the door. He lowered his voice as someone approached the shop. "You sure you *want* the divorce?"

"What kind of question is that? Of course I do. I wanted it five *years* ago."

The bells above the door clamored, drawing Laurel's attention to the new arrivals. A pair of teenage girls approached the counter. Their Instagram-worthy outfits and styled hair and makeup made them look sorely out of place, but Laurel wasn't surprised they were here. They'd ask to rent a couple of kayaks, but what they really wanted was Cody's attention, however briefly they might get it. Never mind that he was twenty-seven and they were still in high school. Her brother attracted all ages from those boy-crazy teens to the oldest member of the local book club.

With his effortless charm, he could talk a woman deathly afraid of water into a kayak with hardly more than a smile.

"I think you're second-guessing yourself or you wouldn't have told me," he said to Laurel before turning his attention to his new customers. "How can I help you ladies?"

"We want to rent a couple of kayaks," said the one with chocolate brown hair styled in cascading waves. Laurel wondered if the poor girl realized how quickly her eyeshadow would be ruined. The waters were calm near the shop, but not too far from shore, small waves would crash into the boat, rocking and splashing. Would she still be all smiles when the curl was drenched right out of style?

"Ever kayaked before?" Cody asked, professional as ever. The female attention never fazed him. He only lived in Sunset Ridge for the season; as soon as the last kayak was put up for the year, he'd be on a plane to his next exotic adventure. She missed him like crazy when he was half a world away.

So would any girl who was foolish enough to fall for him.

"Laurel, why don't you take a kayak out?" Cody suggested. "Might do you good to get some fresh air."

"Yeah, I think you're right."

Laurel left her brother inside with his new fan club while she pit-stopped at the restroom to make sure she wouldn't regret the coffee. Then she grabbed a paddle and headed toward the remaining kayaks on shore. She hadn't packed any snacks or lunch, but she didn't have that kind of time today. She'd asked Ava to meet her at the house for lunch while Mom was out, and rescheduling would only delay the inevitable confession.

A quick, leisurely paddle on mostly calm waters would have to be enough to help silence the loud thoughts bouncing around in her head. It was much preferable to going to Chase's house and sorting through old boxes. She'd put that off as long as she could get away with it.

"Only got two singles left, and I think those are about to be taken. Busy day today," Cody said to his customers. Or so Laurel thought until she heard his voice.

"Want to ride tandem, Laurel?"

She spun, her wide eyes quickly narrowing at the intrusion. "What're you doing here?"

Chase stood next to Cody, wearing that crooked smile that always softened her, no matter how irritated she might be. It wasn't fair. "I'm renting a kayak."

"Are you following me?"

"How could I? I didn't know you'd be here."

Laurel folded her arms over her chest as her brother joined her on the sand, pulling the last two single-passenger kayaks off to the side. All ideas of a peaceful morning flew away with the morning breeze. "I thought you had a job," she said to Chase.

"Took comp time this morning for working the fire the other night."

"Of course you did," she muttered under her breath.

"These things don't just happen," Cody said quietly to Laurel, his insightful advice right on time for Chase's untimely arrival. But whether he was referring to sharing a kayak or missing a signature, she didn't get a chance to ask before two teenage girls emerged from the shop.

"We're ready!" the blonde one announced, her dangly earring making a racket as she bounced in excitement.

"You might want to take out your earrings," Laurel called to her.

"Why?"

"She's right," Cody added, his suave words drawing the teens' full attention. Her brother only had to speak a single word to put a girl in a trance. *Pathetic.* "Be a bad deal if they got caught on anything."

The blonde promptly removed her earrings without another word and shoved them in her purse. Laurel didn't bother to mention she needed a water-proof bag. Her brother could handle his fan club just fine.

"Get me out of here," Laurel muttered.

"Gladly." Chase brushed passed her, pushing the front edge of a tandem kayak into the water. He slipped into the back of it.

It wasn't impossible to take a tandem kayak by oneself, but Laurel knew from experience that it wasn't ideal. They could be harder to steer if the waves were too strong. "We ride like we did last night," she barked a low order at him in passing.

"With you doing all the talking?" Chase teased.

Cody's shoulders shook in laughter as she slipped into the front of the kayak, already regretting agreeing to this. She could compartmentalize her emotions better than most, but each minute spent with Chase threatened to disrupt her whole system. *Five days. Just five more days.* But with Cody's latest insightful words of wisdom to ponder on, Laurel wasn't certain she'd last that long. "I only have an hour," she said over her shoulder to Chase.

"Me, too."

Together, they pushed off the shore. As promised, Chase stayed quiet as the shore disappeared. Laurel relaxed her tense shoulders, letting his paddle do most of the work now that they were far away from Cody's fan club. She relished in the silence and dramatic Alaskan scenery surrounding them. Moments like these, she couldn't remember why she ever left this behind.

"Does Zeus like the water?" Laurel asked after several blissful minutes of solitude.

"Not really." Chase laughed. "You should see him when he steps in a puddle. That dog becomes the biggest princess I've ever met."

Laurel didn't bother to fight her smile. He couldn't see it anyway. Chase had always wanted a dog. They'd planned to pick one out together from the local shelter, but before they could, their world turned upside down. A stray tear rolled down Laurel's cheek, but she didn't dare wipe it away. She didn't want Chase to know she was anything more than a-okay.

"Busy tonight?" Chase asked after several minutes of silence.

"What part of *no talking* confuses you?"

"You started it."

"My baby sister had a baby. I'm busy every night for at least the next couple of years. Probably longer."

"Haylee has a mother," Chase pointed out. "One who's not you."

"Have you *met* my mother?"

"Yes, and she's terrific."

"Well, she overwhelms Haylee. That's why I moved back. To help keep the peace."

"Is that your plan?" Chase asked, his tone more curious than judgmental. "Live with your parents until Haylee either gets married or Melly goes off to college?"

In truth, Laurel hadn't given much thought to her living situation since she moved back. Living on her own had been out of the question while Haylee was pregnant. Her sister needed a buffer when Mom prodded too much or Dad threatened to hunt down the *punk* who knocked her up. Cody had only come back for the season a couple of weeks before Melly was born, and he'd leave in the fall.

Naturally, it made sense that Laurel live with the rest of her family. For how long, she hadn't figured that part out.

"So what if I do?" She didn't mean it. It was one thing to be twenty-nine and living with her parents *temporarily*. But to be in her thirties or forties? *Yikes!* She made a mental note to contact the local realtor, Jolene Davies. Ask her to keep an eye out for something cozy and affordable, for informational purposes should she need it. Enough for her to make an eventual plan. But it would still be several weeks, if not months, before Laurel felt comfortable leaving Haylee on her own.

"What aren't you telling everybody?" Chase challenged.

"What—" She cut herself off because she remembered the email with the incredibly tempting offer from her old boss. If money was her main motivator, she'd be a fool to turn it down. She could amass a small fortune with the clients he promised to give her if she returned to the Florida Keys. Though it was certainly a consideration, Laurel didn't think she'd accept it.

"Laurel, when are you going to learn that secrets are not necessarily a good thing?"

Maneuvering around low-hanging branches, a small rocky island with a few trees sprouting from its jagged surface appeared in front of them. Laurel steered left, but Chase went right. Chase was too strong for their own good.

"Turn!" Laurel yelled at him as the rocky island grew frighteningly close. "The other way!"

Laurel squeezed her eyes shut, bracing for impact. But the crash never came. She opened one cautious eye, catching Chase pushing off the rocky wall with his paddle. "You think this is my first time out?"

"Not funny."

"I thought it was quite entertaining."

He was trying to rile her up, but she wasn't going to let him any more than he already had. "We need to head back," Laurel insisted. "I have to meet your sister for lunch so I can tell her we're still married. How's that for *not* keeping secrets?"

Several beats filled with only the whooshing of water and cries of nearby seagulls caused Laurel to turn her head over her shoulder at Chase. "*Now* you're speechless?"

"Have you told her—"

"No. And I'm not going to." Why she kept the miscarriage so close to the vest five years later, she could no longer say. *Embarrassment? Fear of pity? Unwillingness to deal with the despairing grief all over again?* Whatever the true reason, she wasn't ready to divulge that secret. "But if Ava finds out we're still hitched from anyone but me, I'll be uninvited to her wedding."

They steered around the small island, turning back toward the kayak rental shop. Passing the teens who were stopped in the water, taking selfies. Laurel shook her head, hoping they didn't lose a phone. The water was fairly deep in this area, and gentle waves crashed into the side of their kayaks every few seconds. If they dropped one, they weren't getting it back without scuba gear.

Laurel almost warned them, but thought better of it. If she startled them, they might drop the phone anyway.

She was almost sad when Chase tugged the kayak onto shore. Despite their bickering, she'd be lying if she said she hadn't enjoyed the time spent together. As social as they both were, she'd always loved the moments spent in comfortable silence the most. It was so much easier to lie to herself than face the truth.

I blame Cody and his stupid words of wisdom.

"Think you could stop by tonight?" Chase asked after they returned the paddles. "To go through those boxes. Before you say you're too busy, I'll grill steaks."

"Ribeyes?" Laurel asked, her eyebrow raised.

"The juiciest, fattiest ones I can get my hands on."

Laurel should say no. Make *any* excuse to avoid this task until she could add her missing signature to the papers. But a steak sounded so much better than squabbling over leftovers at home while Mom was at her book club. "If you overcook it, I'm out."

"That's fair."

They stood awkwardly on the steep incline, Chase on the sand, Laurel on the grass. The hill put them at eyelevel. Both searching for words, but neither finding the right ones. "I need to talk to Cody," Laurel finally said.

"I need to pay for my rental," Chase added, following her to the door.

"He's not going to charge you," Laurel said as they stepped inside, interrupting a conversation between her brother and a man in a white collared shirt and tan slacks. His belly bulged a good deal over his belt. If she had to guess, she would say he was in his mid-to-late forties.

"Chase, this gentleman says he's looking for you."

Laurel read nothing but confusion on Chase's mostly blank expression as he stepped forward. "Can I help you?"

"Chase Monroe?"

Chase nodded.

"I'm Tuck Granger. Insurance adjuster. Just had a couple questions for you about that cabin fire. The one on"—he lifted his clipboard, reading off the address—"1547 Jack Rabbit Creek Road."

For the briefest of moments, Chase looked back at Laurel and they shared a gaze that spoke volumes.

A language only the two of them could understand. Laurel didn't know much about structure fires, but something about this strange man in town raised the hairs on the back of her neck. Chase sensed it too. She could read it in his eyes.

"Say six tonight?" Chase said to Laurel.

"Okay."

Chase led the insurance adjuster out the door, leaving her alone with Cody.

"What is that about?" Cody asked.

Ordinarily, Laurel told Cody everything. If there was one person she had no secrets from, it was him. But this wasn't hers to share. "I'm not entirely sure," she finally answered. "But something tells me it's not good."

"Sis?"

Laurel tore her gaze from the front door and dropped it on Cody. "Yeah?"

"Be careful."

"About this or Chase?"

Cody's expression was far too serious to provide much comfort. "Both."

Chapter Six

CHASE

Chase raised the sledgehammer, ready to bust through the back of the closet wall. He probably hadn't watched enough YouTube videos to take the swing, but he'd decided on a larger guest suite and the wall had to come down one way or another. The end result would give his parents a place they could stay when they visited Sunset Ridge. Ava would thank him tenfold for that.

Watching too many online videos was only keeping him from bringing his vision to life. Or perhaps they were robbing him of the joy of smashing through a wall. He felt certain it would make him feel better to take a few swings.

"Stand back, Zeus," Chase said, holding the sledgehammer over his shoulder like a baseball bat. Mid-swing, Zeus started barking. Chase fought to pull back his swing, but the unstoppable force put a small hole in the wall anyway.

The pup ran circles around the room whining excitedly, periodically stopping at the window.

"Laurel here?" He'd lost track of time after he picked up the steaks. It was only by a miracle that he avoided Glenn today. The chief would be upset with him for delaying his inspection report another day, but he couldn't in good conscience sign off on it as-is.

The old shack having insurance at all was mind-boggling.

What company would even insure such a place? It was a losing bet, and from his experience, insurance companies rarely took on losing bets without wildly high premiums. He couldn't imagine *any* company insuring that shack Tuck Granger had called a cabin. That red flag he couldn't so easily ignore. Hopefully Glenn would understand.

Zeus barked boisterously from the hallway half a second before the doorbell rang, forcing Chase to set aside his conspiracy theory for later. Laurel was what mattered now.

He raced down the upstairs hall, stopping so fast he nearly tripped over his own two feet outside the nursery. The cedar log crib he built for their child—the same crib she'd never seen—was in that room. He'd almost gifted it to Haylee until he saw the new crib she posted on her Instagram. Laurel couldn't see it. Not tonight. Maybe not ever.

The door didn't always latch which was why Zeus had probably pushed it open with his snoopy nose. Chase had been meaning to replace the doorknob mechanism, and made a mental note to do it soon. He pulled the nursery door closed and raced downstairs to answer the front door, pulling it open at the same time Laurel rang the doorbell a second time.

"Hey," he said, slightly out of breath. "Come in."

"I brought wine." She held a bottle of merlot in offering as she stepped inside the home they'd once called *theirs*. "Not sure if you can drink it—"

"Bauer's on call tonight. Not me." He followed her to the kitchen, an aching in his chest at the familiarity of it all. She belonged here. With him. In the house they picked out together. The one they had talked about filling with kids and dogs. And most importantly, love. It was supposed to be their forever home.

"Why are you wearing goggles on top of your head?" Laurel asked, setting the wine on the counter.

"Oh, the renovation project. The one I told you about."

"You didn't actually say much about it."

Chase waved a dismissive hand. "Early stages yet. Your boxes are in the dining room. But we can wait until after dinner—"

"No, I'm ready now."

It felt as though she were rushing him, but the bottle of wine said otherwise. "I can let you get started with all that and fire up the grill," Chase offered, too confused to sort out her signals. He blamed the insurance adjuster for taking up too much space in his already crowded mind. "The steaks have been resting long enough to put them on." The nervousness was frustrating. He'd felt it plenty when they first started dating. Maybe even more now that there was much more at stake than winning another date. Their whole future hung in the balance, and so far, his plan to win his wife back was mediocre at best. *At least she showed up.* "Steaks if you're hungry now. Or I can wait."

"I'm starving, actually."

Chase was about to lead her to the dining room but caught himself and grabbed the plate of seasoned steaks instead. Never mind that the grill wasn't even on yet, much less warmed up to temp. "You know where it is."

"Yes, I do." She offered him a kind, fleeting smile. "But I might take a glass of wine with me."

Chase set down the plate and fished out a bottle opener from the back of a very cluttered drawer of random utensils. Before he could secure the bottle, Laurel touched his hand. His body froze as shivers of electricity raced up his arm and warmed his whole chest. "I can do that," Laurel offered, seemingly unaffected by their touch.

"Right." He handed the bottle opener over. "C'mon, Zeus. Let's get the steaks on." The pup looked back and forth between them, his decision heavy. It was likely the aroma of raw steak—not Chase's company—he finally chose. "Medium rare?" he asked at the kitchen door that led to the backyard.

"Is there any other way to eat a steak?"

That's my girl.

So far this night was going nothing as Chase had carefully planned when he first thought up the excuse. He'd been too caught up in his own thoughts about work to be prepared beyond seasoning steaks.

He intended to be with Laurel when she went through her things. To offer moral support, share laughs from happy memories, and wipe away her tears when they came.

Yet he was out at the grill, babysitting steaks, watching her back through the window.

"I'm screwing this all up, boy," he said to Zeus. "Got any bright ideas to turn this around?"

The sliding door to the deck opened. "Thought you might want a glass, too." She set the half-filled glass near the steaks. He wondered if she'd found the wine glasses tucked in the back of his cupboards or in one of her boxes. He certainly hadn't used them since she left.

"Wow!" Laurel stepped off the deck and into the landscaped backyard, Zeus following at her heel. "You've done so much since I . . ." She let her words trail off as she stepped onto the elaborate stone patio area. It'd taken him half a summer to complete the firepit project she'd dreamed up. One that could comfortably seat a dozen or more people around a fire. "You did all this?"

"I forced Ryder to work for beer on occasion." With the gas grill at temp, Chase set the steaks on, relishing in the sizzle. That was the sound of a happy summer right there.

"You didn't hire this out?" Laurel pressed, staring at him as if he might have grown a tail.

He chuckled at her disbelief. "No, I swear."

"Let me guess. You learned all of this from YouTube."

Chase shrugged, reaching for the glass of wine. They used to share part of a bottle over dinner a couple nights a week. Laurel would pick out the kind and he would use his best grilling skills to create a meal worthy of it. "I may have watched a couple, yeah."

Laurel sat on one of the stone benches. He couldn't read her expression with the way her blonde waves curtained her cheek. When they first looked at this house, they talked about creating a firepit area. One where they could host their friends. It didn't get nearly the attention it deserved, outside of Chase keeping the weeds out of it.

"Can't burn any fires right now," he said, mostly to keep conversation flowing.

"Too dry?"

"Yeah. Chief announced a ban yesterday."

"It's really a good thing that fire was put out before it did some serious damage."

"Good thing for sure." Her comment sent his mind right back to work. To the unsigned investigation report, to the insurance adjuster, and Henry Davenport's coincidental luck being out at the property at just the right time to call in the fire before it got out of control.

"I can't believe you built this," Laurel said, pulling him back to the present. "Why aren't we having Ava's birthday cookout here?"

Chase lifted his hands in surrender. "I offered. She wanted to use her own, even though it's half the size." The mention of his sister reminded him of the lunch Laurel was supposed to have with her today. "Did you tell her?" he asked when she stepped back onto the deck in search of her wine glass.

"Yeah, I told her."

"How did she take it?" He'd missed a call from Ava earlier, but because she hadn't left a voicemail or sent him a text, he hadn't called her back. Until now, he hadn't considered that it might be about the unexpected news of him still being hitched.

"She's still talking to me, so there's that." Laurel's tone lacked enthusiasm. "But of course it reminded her of me leaving—"

"Why don't you tell them, Laurel?" Chase asked delicately, knowing full well his unwelcome question might send her running before he even flipped the steaks. "They're your best friends. They'll understand why you left."

"And why I kept it a secret? No, thanks." Laurel shook her head before she emptied her wine glass. "I'll be inside, going through my boxes." Zeus trotted after her, hedging his bets on Laurel's pets against Chase giving him steak handouts from a closed grill.

Leaving Chase alone in the backyard once again.

He flipped the steaks.

He'd been hurt, too. Losing a child he'd never been granted the opportunity to meet cut deeper than any pain he'd ever experienced, more so when Laurel left him to deal with it alone. He couldn't imagine carrying that same child and losing it. Why did it matter if people knew? That, he would never understand.

Chase watched Laurel through the window, her attention given more to Zeus than to the stack of boxes, which was just fine with him. If she didn't get through it all tonight, she'd have a reason to come back. Or better yet, to come home.

A loud sizzle warned him he was forgetting the steaks. It would be just his luck to overcook them after the way this night had gone already. He plated them and crossed his fingers as he carried them inside. It was only once he was in the kitchen that he realized he hadn't prepared any sides.

He didn't have so much as a scrap of lettuce to offer.

"Something wrong?" Laurel asked from the opposite side of the breakfast bar as he frantically searched through cupboards for a can of baked beans or a bag of chips. He really needed to stop eating out so much and buy real groceries.

"No sides."

Laurel shrugged. "I'm really only hungry for steak anyway."

"I'm sorry—"

"Chase, it's fine." Her tone was firm and compassionate. "I imagine that insurance adjuster has your mind preoccupied."

"You could say that."

She slid into a bar stool and leaned her elbows on the counter, watching him slice both steaks into strips like he used to do on evenings like these. Her gentle smile made him cautiously optimistic that this night wasn't complete a loss. "What did he want anyway?"

Chase debated answering her question too openly. Professionally speaking, he shouldn't discuss the case with anyone not directly involved until it was closed. But Laurel wasn't just anyone. Not to him. "He wanted my report."

"Have you finished it?"

"No."

"Couldn't sign it off, could you?"

"I was going to," Chase admitted, handing her a plate. As much as he wanted to place his next to her, he decided staying on this side of the counter was safer for the way the day had gone thus far. With his luck, he'd go to kiss her and spill wine in both their laps. "I went kayaking to clear my head. To run over the evidence one last time before I finalized it. But that guy showing up is exactly the reason I didn't want to. I knew something was off about all this. Who insures a shack that could've collapsed with a strong gust of wind? It doesn't make sense."

"Did the adjuster tell you anything useful?"

"You think he'd be more helpful. If I hand over my report as-is, they have to pay out the claim. In my experience, those guys try everything they can to pay as little as possible."

"You don't think Henry Davenport did this, do you?"

Chase stabbed a strip of steak with his fork, chewing slowly as he mulled that over. He didn't know the man well, but Henry was a community-involved citizen. Always donated his time to help with setup and teardown of the summer festivals. Hung with the coffee-drinking crowd who still preferred the Moosecakes diner to Black Bear Coffee. Attended church on Sundays. "No, I really don't think Henry did this."

"He couldn't have set the fire anyway, right? If his story holds true." Laurel moaned softly at the next bite of steak, temporarily raising Chase's ego. "I've been to five-star restaurants that can't grill a steak like you can."

"Guess I've still got *some* skills."

They shared a dangerously flirtatious gaze across the breakfast bar. One that begged Chase to shove away the contents between them and kiss Laurel until they were both oxygen-deprived. And maybe even a few seconds more.

Laurel was the first to look away, slipping a piece of steak to Zeus. "Do you believe him? Henry?"

"You think he's lying."

Laurel shrugged. "Seems convenient he was out on that property at just the right time, considering they live down the street from my parents. Can you hunt anything this time of year?"

"Just small game. Pheasants, ptarmigan, that sort of thing."

"I still think it's wrong that you can *hunt* our state bird." She shook her head, reaching for her half-empty wine glass. If she had another, Chase would insist on driving her home. Maybe he would regardless, because he hadn't spotted her car in the driveway. No way he was letting her walk across town alone.

"Henry didn't say anything about hunting," Chase said, thinking back to the very generic statement he provided the police. "He has a right to be on his property, even if there isn't another house or anything on it. Some people go for drives to think or watch the sunset."

"Which is why no one else is questioning it like you are." She carried her empty plate to the sink and rinsed it off before she opened the dishwasher. "Do you even use this thing?"

"Not really."

"Why not?"

Chase shrugged. "Don't dirty many dishes. You were the one who wanted the dishwasher, remember?"

"Because I was the one who *washed* all the dishes."

"Feel free to carry on that tradition tonight," he teased, and she hit him with the towel she used to wipe her hands. Chase grabbed for her wrists, pinning her against the sink as she playfully struggled to get free. Their laughter caused Zeus to bark enthusiastically, pacing behind them trying to figure out how he could join in on the fun.

Chase couldn't stop staring at her wine-stained lips, craving her kiss more than ever. They belonged together. She had to feel it, too. "You remember what happened the last time you whapped me with a towel?"

"Whapped?" Laurel repeated, bursting out in a fit of giggles that made Zeus bark louder. "You said *whapped*."

"And someone is officially tipsy."

"Not even close." She pushed at his chest with her palms flat against him. His heart thundered in his ears. How many nights had he dreamed of being this close to his wife again? With the way her eyes darkened a shade, she might let him kiss her. And he wanted to kiss her. *Badly*.

The echo of the doorbell made Chase want to curse, but he held his tongue. Of all the moments for an interruption, this was the worst. "I can ignore it," he said to Laurel, dropping his gaze to her lips without an ounce of discretion.

"You—you should answer it." Her words were

nearly panted, as if they'd been making out instead of *almost* getting to the good part. "I need to use the restroom."

"Use the one upstairs," Chase said, reluctantly pushing back from the sink and letting Laurel free. "Just trust me on that."

As Laurel hurried up the stairs, Chase went to answer the door. But not before the doorbell abuser got in a series of rings. If it was one of his buddies, he might slug them for the untimely interruption.

"Ava."

"You should try answering your phone."

Chase frowned, certain he had only missed the one call from her earlier today. Maybe she'd tried again when he was focused on Laurel's very kissable lips. But certainly, it wasn't enough to warrant an in-person visit. "You didn't even leave a voicemail. Is there an emergency?"

"No. But that's not the point." Ava stepped forward, fully intended to invite herself inside, but Chase blocked her path. No one, his sister included, was going to stop him from kissing Laurel tonight. *No one.* "You have a date in there or something?"

"Yeah, I do."

Ava raised her eyebrows at him. "Who?"

"My wife." It felt good to say that. *Really* good.

So good his smile stretched his cheeks. "I assume that's why you're here?"

"Yeah, but—"

"I love you, dear sister. But you will have to come back another time. Tonight, I'm busy."

Ava moved her lips a few times, as if she were trying to get words to come out. But after a few attempts, she clamped them shut and simply stared at him.

"I know what I'm doing, if that's what you're worried about," Chase said.

"I wish I believed you."

"If I get hurt again, it's my own fault."

Ava nodded, reluctance heavy in her expression. "I'll call you tomorrow. Try answering your phone when I do."

He could argue that he was busy working, or hurry back to the woman waiting inside. Chase closed the door the moment she turned to leave. A quick scan of the kitchen, living area, and dining room meant Laurel was likely still upstairs.

The absence of clicking claws suggested Zeus was too.

Chase took the stairs two at a time, catching Laurel outside the nursery. The door was open a crack, and Zeus wagged his tail with what Chase could only assume was pride. As if he wanted to show Laurel the door he had bested. "Hey," he said, stopping Laurel with her hand on the knob. Another night he could show her the crib. Tonight was not that night.

"Who was at the door?"

"Ava."

"Is she downstairs?"

Chase closed the distance between them in two quick strides, reaching for Laurel's hand. He tugged her away from the door, backing her up against the wall. Propping his hand beside her cheek. "I told her we were busy." He didn't wait for a response before he swooped his free hand beneath her cheek and drew her lips to his with a gentle, testing brush.

His entire body shivered as her soft lips pressed harder into his and her fingers dug into the back of his neck.

Five years of longing and heartache poured into the deepening kiss, promising Chase that he'd never stopped loving her. In her surrender, he thought he felt the same from her. They'd always had a deeply close connection. The ability to sense what the other was feeling. A connection that was mending and strengthening with each second their lips were joined.

"Stay with me, Laurel," Chase pleaded in a whisper, locking his heated gaze with her own. "I miss my *wife*."

"I can't."

"You can."

"Haylee needs me. Melly too. You know that. I-I should go."

Chase pushed off from the wall, undeniably disappointed. But a sense of hope he hadn't felt before had blossomed. He still had four full days to convince her fate was giving them a second chance, and he wasn't giving up without pulling out all the stops. "C'mon then. I'll take you home."

Chapter Seven

LAUREL

Laurel woke at four twenty-eight in the morning to Melly screaming. But it wasn't why she woke up irritated. Oh no, that honor belonged to one Chase Monroe. How dare he kiss her until her toes curled and her body went limp! How dare he make her *feel* things she swore she'd never feel again.

She pushed herself out of bed to check on Haylee. Some early mornings Laurel found her sister smiling, rocking Melly in the wooden rocker their grandfather had made before Marc was born. Other times, she found her poor sister drowning in a pool of overwhelmed tears.

"Want me to take her?" Laurel offered when she spotted the shine on Haylee's cheeks.

"She doesn't want a bottle. I already changed her diaper. I'm not any good at this." Haylee let out a hiccupping sob. "I love her more than anything else on this earth, but I suck at being her mom."

After checking Melly's forehead, Laurel bounced the baby in her arms, hoping the motion would soothe her crying. Nights like these made Laurel question whether *she* had ever been cut out to be a mom herself. "You don't suck at being her mom," Laurel said softly but sternly enough to be heard over the crying. "You were *meant* to be her mom. It's what fate decided, and fate always has a reason for its choices." The words were harder for Laurel to accept, but she pushed the unwanted emotions down to focus on the present.

"Yeah, right. You mean the way fate decided you're still *married*?"

Laurel's eyes doubled in size as she stretched her neck out into the hall. She hadn't told anyone but Kinley, Ava, and Cody. The last thing she needed was Mom or Dad overhearing that bit of news. Convinced the coast was clear, Laurel lowered her voice. "That's *not* the same thing."

"Is too."

"It's too early for this," Laurel muttered. "Who told you anyway?"

"No one *told* me." Which meant Haylee had been secretly listening in over lunch with Ava yesterday. Laurel thought she was clever, hosting the meeting at the house. Too worried that nosy eavesdroppers in any restaurant might hear her news and spread it all over town.

"Should've known you weren't really taking a nap," Laurel mumbled.

"You got home pretty late. Were you with him last night?"

"None of your business." Thinking about last night—*those kisses*—would only make everything more complicated than it already was. She focused on the angry angel in her arms, trying the rocker with Melly. But nothing seemed to soothe her. "You're sure she's not hungry?"

"Fed her an hour ago. But try for yourself if you don't think I fed her enough." Haylee shoved a bottle at Laurel before adding, "I think you *were* with him tonight. Are you going to get back together?" A new shine of tears glossed in her eyes. "You are, aren't you? You're going to move out and leave me all alone here to deal with everything."

"It's one signature. It'll be final Monday."

Laurel's heart squeezed at her own words. Until those mind-melting kisses, she'd been one hundred percent set on signing that last blank line the minute Jenkins opened his door. There wasn't room for doubt, but it was seeping in anyway. "Just, please don't say anything to Mom or Dad, okay? No need to get everyone worked up over a small technicality."

Haylee folded her arms over her chest. "Unless fate has something to say about it."

Laurel stuck her tongue out, as though they were kids again. "Motherhood has made you a brat."

"A very *tired* brat."

"Everything okay in here?" Mom asked with a yawn, coming into the room and holding her hands out for Melly. "Why are you still crying, baby girl?" Mom's attempt to walk around the room and bounce her lightly did nothing to soothe her screams. "Did you feed her?"

"An hour ago. She's not hungry."

"Diaper change?"

"Ten minutes ago. She doesn't have a fever, in case you're wondering that too."

"You burped her?"

"An hour ago, right after I fed her," Haylee answered with a huff of frustration. "She burped so loud she could put Marc to shame."

Mom reached for the burping cloth and set to the task again. "I think she's a bit gassy. We might need to switch up her formula. She's been awful fussy this week, and that could be why."

"Really?" Haylee seemed on the verge of tears, but whether from guilt or relief, Laurel was too tired and lost in her own thoughts to decipher. Melly belched and her crying finally subsided. "Why are you better at this than I am?" Haylee asked Mom.

"The only reason I look like an expert now is because I made all the mistakes raising the five of you." After setting Melly back in her crib, Mom put an arm around Haylee and pulled her in for a hug. "I'm not your enemy, Haylee. I've just got some experience and wisdom to share. I'm sorry if I come off a little pushy. I'm still adjusting to *my* baby having a baby of her own." She kissed Haylee on the forehead, and Laurel slipped out of the room to let them have their touching moment without her.

Maybe moving out of her parents' house wouldn't be a terrible thing. Haylee wouldn't be alone. She'd be in good hands—the *best* hands. It was time Laurel figured out what came next in her life.

She dropped onto the bed, eager for another hour of sleep. Never in her life had she appreciated silence as much as she did right now. She let her heavy eyelids fall closed, willing good dreams to whisk her away. But before sleep could overtake her, she heard tapping on the glass. If one of her siblings was messing with her, she was going to kill them. Laurel hid her face beneath a pillow, but the tapping didn't stop.

"Ugh!" She threw the pillow off, fully prepared to incinerate the culprit with her fiery glare. Instead, she stifled a scream. A giant moose face peered down at her. Antlers bumped the window creating the annoying tapping she'd heard as Ed tilted his head in what she could only describe as curiosity. "If you think I have more coffee, you're wrong." But of course the moose couldn't hear her through the glass. "What do you want, *Ed*?"

When Laurel moved out, she was going to sleep for a straight week. Anyone who had half a brain wouldn't dare disturb her. Ed included.

The moose didn't leave, and the tapping didn't stop. She threw aside the covers, giving up on sleep. She slipped on her robe, feeling Ed's gaze following her around her basement-level bedroom. *What does he want?* With any luck, Dad might have some coffee brewing.

The kitchen was empty, but the coffee pot was full. She filled her cup and slipped out onto the back deck, unsurprised to find Ed loitering near her bedroom window. Maybe she imagined it, but she swore his ears perked at the cup in her hands. "I don't have enough to share," Laurel said, silently wondering if she was losing her marbles conversating with a moose. "It's not as good as Black Bear, either."

Ed's massive body sauntered through the grass, approaching the deck. With each step closer, he seemed to double in size.

"You can't come up here," she told him, eyeing the sliding door as her hands shook slightly. "You'll bust through the boards. You're too heavy."

Ed dipped his head near the base of the steps, sniffing something in the grass.

"You're really odd, you know that?"

He lifted his head, reminding her he could scoop her up with his antlers. He might be a local favorite and a bit quirky, but he was still a wild animal capable of causing a person a great deal of harm if he felt threatened. Laurel shuffled back slowly, creating extra distance between them.

"Don't you have a girlfriend to woo? Or maybe you're running *from* her," she added in a chuckle. "Look, I don't believe any of the rumors about your matchmaking antics are true. I think people read too much into things because they want to believe in something that makes them forget how rotten the world can be. So you can stop trying to be my fairy god moose or whatever."

Ed tilted his head at her.

"I know you don't understand a single word I'm saying, but I'm glad my voice intrigues you." She glanced down at the nearly full cup steaming between her hands. "Or maybe you have a new affinity for coffee because of me."

The moose kicked at the ground beneath the deck steps, causing Laurel to freeze. Was he going to *charge* her?

At some sound Laurel couldn't detect, Ed froze. Much like a dog catching the distant sound of a familiar engine or rustle in the trees. Seconds later, the moose turned away and trotted off into the heavy tree line as if he were being chased.

"Weird moose."

The sliding door opened, and Dad stepped out to join her, his own cup in hand. "You couldn't sleep either?"

"Seemed pointless to go back to bed after all that," Laurel said, omitting any detail about Ed. She leaned over the deck railing, the rising sun catching something shiny at the foot of the steps. She refused to believe Ed was trying to point it out. He was probably just as curious about the shiny object as she was. "I'll be at the store a couple hours this morning."

"Sounds good."

She descended the three steps to get a better look at the shiny object, certain it was a dime or something equally unexciting. "Maybe sometime soon we can discuss a more permanent arrangement. You'll be looking for an assistant manager soon, right?"

"You're not going to take your old boss up on his offer, then?"

Dad was the only one who knew about the dilemma. Chase was right, she sure had a lot of secrets. The weight of them continued to pile on. It was the reason she decided today was the day. She was going to come clean to her best friends about the reason she left. The miscarriage, her begging Chase to keep the secret, all of it. Even the painful stuff she wouldn't admit to herself.

"I'm home to stay, Dad. I don't want to move back to Florida. The money doesn't entice me."

"You know we'll gladly have you as long as you want to stay—"

"I'll find my own place soon." She bent down, gasping when she saw it was a ring. *Her* ring. A white gold wedding band bonded to a beautiful diamond engagement ring. The unique way they intertwined left no doubt. What in the world was it doing out here?

"Anything interesting?" Dad asked.

She dropped the ring in her robe pocket. "Just a dime." *Another secret, Laurel. Great idea.* It puzzled her why her ring was outside instead of tucked away in her jewelry case where she last put it, but Laurel had enough things to worry about without allowing Ed's mischief to add to them. "I'm going to grab a shower." She patted Dad on the arm. "I'll see you at the store."

"Do you remember the crazy things I used to be talked into doing because of these darn scones?" Ava broke off a piece of blueberry scone, shaking her head in reminiscent laughter. "You guys got me in so much trouble. I spent half my junior high and high school years grounded, and there was always a scone to blame."

Kinley pointed a piece of broken scone at Ava from across the booth. "No one *made* you go along with anything."

"But we weren't going to leave you out, either,"

Laurel added, nudging Ava with her shoulder. "Let's be honest."

It felt good to laugh together in one of their old hangouts, Bonita's Bakery. The scones were legendary and trance-inducing delicious. The atmosphere was fun and upbeat with the bright teal-blue walls and pink cartoonish cupcake decorations scattered throughout. Laurel didn't have any bad memories here. Which was the reason she picked this location over any other.

She waited until the elderly Jones twins abandoned their table. Aside from Bonita and her daughter working in the kitchen, the three of them were alone.

Laurel knew it was now or she'd lose her nerve all over again before the next customer walked in.

"I need to tell you both something, and it won't be easy for me." She fiddled with a napkin, studying the donut patterns on it so she could avoid their curious gazes. "I don't want your pity. It's far too late for that, and it'll only upset me. No questions would be preferable, but I'll understand if you have a couple."

"Are you thinking about staying married to Chase?" Ava asked, reminding Laurel that Ava had been shooed away from her brother's house last night, and as a result, she sent a dozen text messages to Laurel this morning. Ones she'd ignored, blaming work. "You are, aren't you?"

From Ava's tone, Laurel couldn't tell if that idea excited or upset her best friend. Because whichever was the case, the opposite would be true when she admitted she was going to sign as planned come Monday. Bravely she looked up, but was unable to read the answer in Ava's neutral expression. "This isn't about that, exactly."

Kinley rested her hand on top of Laurel's. "Hey, we're your best friends. Here for you no matter what."

"Right," Ava agreed without missing a beat. "I'm not really wearing the best shoes to hide a body, but if that's what you need us to do, I'm in."

Reassurance washed over Laurel like a warm blanket. This was the right thing to do, even if it forced her to confront emotions she preferred to keep buried. "It's about the reason I left." With a deep breath, she unleashed the truth she'd been holding onto so fiercely. "We were pregnant. We were going to wait until I made it to the second trimester to tell everyone. Only, I never did. I had a miscarriage. A really bad one." *Blood. So much blood.* Memories of that horrid night plagued her with rapid succession, and it took extra strength to shut them out. "I wasn't the same after that. I was broken inside. Embarrassed. Ashamed. Stricken with grief. I felt like such a failure. I *still* feel a lot of those feelings. It . . . sticks with you."

"So you left." Kinley's tone didn't hold an ounce of judgment.

"It was like a dream shattered, and I needed a whole new life." She waited for Ava to say something about her abandoning Chase, but instead her friends surrounded her on both sides, gathering her into a tight, oxygen-depriving hug. With their love and support flowing through her veins, she clung to their collective strength and let her emotions loose.

The tears felt liberating.

"I'm not sure why you felt you couldn't tell us," Ava said gently, "but we're glad you shared it with us now."

"There's one more thing." Fear gripped Laurel's entire body at the words she was about to speak. Words she hadn't even allowed herself to think, much less say out loud. "After the miscarriage . . . the doctor . . . I can't have kids."

Her friends hugged her tighter, their tears joining her own. Years of distance hadn't caused them to forget how much the dream of having a large family meant to her. Maybe now they'd understand why she couldn't stay married to Chase.

"I have to sign the papers," she said softly, in defeat. "Chase deserves someone who can give him the family he wants." All this would've been so much easier to stomach had Chase found someone else to settle down with after she left. *Except we'd still be legally married anyway, which would've been awkward.* "Don't try to change my mind on this. And please, don't tell him. I've—I've never told anyone what I just told you both."

"He deserves to know," Ava gently insisted.

Laurel inhaled deeply, fighting a new round of tough tears. "I know. I'll tell him. Just, not yet. I need some time, okay?"

"Of course." Kinley squeezed her tight again. "We love you, Laurel."

"We're here for you," Ava added. "That's what being best friends is all about."

Chapter Eight

CHASE

"I just got off the phone with Mr. Granger." Chief Bauer filled the doorway to their shared office, staring hard at Chase. His face was red, making his thin sandy hair seem even lighter than usual. "You *still* haven't signed off on that report?"

Chase hit the save button on his spreadsheet, taking his time to fully face Glenn. He'd been expecting backlash for his delay, but he was determined to stand his ground. That was the job, after all. He wouldn't rush this until he could gather *all* the facts and evidence. "You don't think it's strange that there's an insurance claim on that shack?"

"Odd," Glenn agreed, folding his arms, then unfolding them and marching toward the coffee pot. "Odd, but not entirely unheard of. Some of these companies insure properties for decades and never come out to see how they deteriorate. You forget, ten or more years ago, that *shack* had renters in it."

"We were going to use the place as a training exercise last year," Chase added, turning full circle in his chair to face Glenn. Zeus crept out of his hole beneath the desk, large ears perked, no doubt on treat-alert. "If they kept insurance on that place, you'd think they would've canceled it then considering we were planning to burn it down."

Glenn stirred a heaping spoonful of sugar into his coffee. "What are you suggesting?"

"That something doesn't add up."

"What evidence do you have to support that theory?"

Chase dug a treat out of his desk drawer and tossed it to Zeus. "No evidence yet, but—"

"We work with facts, Chase. This isn't a mystery novel." Glenn gulped his coffee, making Chase's own throat burn as he watched. Glenn seemed unaffected by the steaming-hot liquid. "I'm tired of being hounded by everyone for that report. Even Evelynn

Marsh is calling me, wanting quotes about this conspiracy you've dredged up."

"Seems over the top, even for a newspaper reporter. Though it's probably the most exciting thing to happen in town for a while."

"Exciting isn't my choice word." Glenn cleared his throat and took another gulp. "The point is that this thing is blowing way out of proportion. The longer you take, the more conspiracy theories float around town. People start making unfair accusations. You've never seen that happen here, but I have. It can get ugly. This town doesn't need *ugly*." Glenn sat on the edge of a metal desk. "I know you're trying to do the right thing, Chase. Being thorough is important."

"That's what I'm doing," he said before the chief could add a *but* to his statement. "Things don't add up, and I want to make sense of them before I sign off. It's my name on that report, and I want to feel right about signing it."

"Understood." Glenn pushed up from the desk, heading for the door. "I want that report finished no later than end of day Monday, or I'm taking over the investigation myself."

Zeus grumbled, almost as if on cue, and dropped back against his bed. Probably because Glenn hadn't come in with a treat as he so often did. But it did give the men a reason to chuckle, breaking through the icy tension. They'd made a solid team these past five years. Chase didn't want this investigation to insert ripples. A divided chief and deputy chief didn't bode well for the department.

"There's one thing that I thought was especially odd," Chase added before Glenn could disappear down the hall.

"What's that?"

"Granger won't tell me what the claim amount is. He seemed secretive about it."

Glenn shrugged. "On that old shack, I doubt it was more than the replacement cost of an outbuilding. Ten, twenty grand at most?"

"Then why doesn't he just tell me that?"

Glenn looked about to answer when his attention was pulled down the hallway Chase couldn't see from his seat. "Police Chief Grant, to what do we owe the pleasure?" Glenn leaned forward, extending his hand before Ryder came into view. It was likely Ryder was here to talk about fishing or something unrelated to the case, but Chase could ask for his help with a couple of things while he was around.

"I'm not here to arrest anyone." Glenn cackled at some inside joke the two of them shared. "Just wanted to drop by and let you know the state patrol picked up a female hitchhiker near Girdwood. She admitted to being this far south and *seeing* the fire. Said she couldn't call it in because she doesn't own a phone. But that's all they could get out of her. She claims she wasn't even on the property, just walking up the highway."

Glenn turned a stern, knowing look to Chase. "What do you know about that?"

"Catching a hitchhiker isn't evidence," Chase argued.

"You're still convinced there's something shady going on?" Ryder asked, coming into the office to greet an eager Zeus. The dog sniffed his pant legs, no doubt detecting his *girlfriend*, Rowdy. The pup would be over the moon at seeing her tomorrow at Ava's birthday cookout. One that was now being hosted in *his* backyard according to his sister's earlier text. He suspected Laurel was behind it, but didn't have time to think too much about all that right now.

No matter how strongly her kisses buzzed on his lips.

"I have some errands to run," Glenn said, dismissing himself.

"That fishing invite is still open," Ryder called after him. "Kings are biting. Just say when."

"Think you can do me a favor?" Chase asked once he heard the door between the offices and the bay close. "Think you can find out how much the insurance claim is on that Jack Rabbit Creek Road property? The adjuster is being extra secretive with me about it."

"Maybe he doesn't want to influence your findings," Ryder suggested.

Chase stared at the coffee pot, considering pouring himself a cup. But there wasn't enough sugar to make it taste half decent even if he was desperate enough to drink it. He'd tossed and turned last night over both the case and Laurel, but preferred an energy drink over too-strong coffee. "Have you ever known an adjuster who didn't try to poke holes? An accidental fire means they have to pay out the claim in full, right?"

"I'll see what I can find out," Ryder finally relented.

"Thanks." It didn't feel like a win. Usually, he and Ryder were on the same wavelength when it came to these things, and when they weren't, it was Ryder who was convinced foul play was at hand and Chase trying—and failing—to convince him he was looking too hard at something simple.

Your gut's never wrong.

Laurel's confidence in him was the only reason he hadn't signed off on that report to please everyone else. Once Ryder left, he'd reexamine the photos. *Something* had to stand out. If he could just find one shred of evidence to support his theory, Glenn would back off. Maybe Ryder would believe him.

"Thought I might take the boat up north this weekend," Ryder said. "Kings are biting, and my freezer is empty. Interested?"

For the first time in longer than he could remember, salmon fishing held almost no appeal to Chase. Leaving town this weekend meant he'd lose valuable time with Laurel. Not that he was doing a stellar job so far. *Except all that kissing. That was progress, right?*

"What's that smirk about?" Ryder accused.

"I can't go this weekend. I've got a wife to win back."

"Oh, right, the ticking clock and all that." Ryder's phone chimed in his shirt pocket. Judging by his smile, it was Kinley. "If you'll excuse me, I'm late for a lunch break."

"The insurance claim," Chase called out to him when Ryder stepped into the hall. "Just need a dollar amount."

"I'll get you your number."

Chase barely navigated to the folder on his computer that held the photos from the scene when Zeus popped to his feet, whining eagerly. Before Chase could soothe the dog, he darted out the door. *Unusual.* He waited several seconds, unsure where the dog could get off to with all the doors closed, including the one to the bay.

"I really like what you've done with your greeting committee." The angelic sound of Laurel's voice temporarily erased all the frustrations of his day thus far. "Of course, he might've smelled the scones."

"Scones?" Chase perked up. "What kind of scones?"

"Blueberry."

His favorite. Though, they were most locals' favorite because Bonita picked the blueberries herself. Every bakery item she sold was moan-worthy delicious, but her blueberry scones were on a level all their own. They could make a man forget his name, they were *that* good. "Pull up a seat."

Laurel set the bag of scones on his desk and went for a chair. "You finish your report?"

"You're the third person to ask me that today. Fourth if you count the adjuster bugging Glenn about it." He watched Laurel break off a corner of her scone, jealous of the crumbs that grazed her lips. He wanted to forget about the report, about the scones, about reality, and draw her into his arms.

More than anything, he wanted their old life back the way it was before everything went south. They couldn't recover their loss, but they could try again. He definitely wanted to try again.

"Stop looking at me like that," she teased.

"Like what?"

"Like I'm some kind of dessert."

"You're better than a dessert, sweetheart."

He tucked his victorious smile out of sight at her blush and enlarged the scene photos on his monitor. "I'm getting more pressure to get this turned in. I shouldn't be sharing these with you, but you're the only one who thinks I'm onto something. Maybe you can spot something I missed."

What he really wanted was an excuse for Laurel to scoot closer, and she did. But Zeus crawled awkwardly into her lap, wobbling a bit on his paws as he balanced his fifty-pound frame on her thighs until he curled into a steady ball, ignoring any objections from Chase about being a lap dog. Laurel didn't mind a bit. Once settled, she stroked Zeus' neck, leaning over him slightly to study the photos.

"I wish I knew what I was looking for."

"Anything that jumps out. Anything that seems odd to you." Their knees brushed, and Laurel didn't pull away from his touch. He pretended not to notice as he leaned closer to the monitor, pointing out the different things he'd noted from the scene. They spent over an hour combing through photos, enlarging areas at times when she thought she caught a glimpse of something odd, but ultimately coming up empty.

"I don't think you're wrong," Laurel said. "But I don't know if you're going to find anything to back you up. Whoever did this must've thought it through. Covered their tracks."

"Tracks," he muttered with an annoyed shake of his head. "The ground's so dry up there that even the tracks from fighting the fire didn't stick. I searched the woods nearby. Nothing. No tracks in there, no discarded kerosene containers. Not even any trash since the high school track team cleaned the area two weeks ago."

"Guessing the fire burned everything inside the cabin, then?"

Chase reached for the Ziploc-bagged items on the opposite side of the monitor. "All I have are some scraps of paper so small I can't tell what they're from.

And a lipstick case. Chief laughed himself hoarse over that one."

Laurel took the clear bag with the black and silver lipstick dispenser in it, examining it closer. "This is expensive."

A beacon of hope hit Chase squarely in the chest at Laurel's interest, but he didn't dare get too excited. "Expensive, how?"

"This black part, that's crocodile leather."

"You're kidding."

"No. Where did you find it, exactly?"

Chase zoomed in on one of the photos, pointing to the pile of rubble near where the only door in and out of the cabin used to be. "I figured it was far enough away from the hottest point of the fire to melt. But knowing it's leather...it takes a lot to burn real leather. Crocodile, you said?" Throat dry from the scones, Chase reached for a mostly empty bottle of water, intending to drain it.

"Yeah. They make these in France, I think. I've never bought one myself. They're like three hundred dollars."

Chase nearly spit out his water, choking on the last bit of it. Zeus looked up in concern, whining softly and licking his hand until he got himself under control. "Three *hundred*, you said?"

"Yeah. See those double hearts? That's the emblem for the brand. I can't remember the name offhand, but I can look it up. I doubt a hitchhiker would've had this on them. You can't resell it or anything. It's lipstick." Laurel made a gross face, causing him to chuckle. "Anyway, I think this is your important clue."

His heavy sigh drew her full attention. "Anyone could've dropped that there in the last ten years."

She lifted the bag, holding the silver bottom of the lipstick canister up for them to see together. "They usually inscribe the year—yep, there it is. This one was made this year." The way Laurel lit up with excitement made him wish this piece of evidence was important. He didn't want to rob her of that joy. "I guess you don't have a way to see who purchased expensive lipstick, huh?"

"Not exactly a database monitoring that, no."

Setting the lipstick evidence bag back on the desk, she picked up the other one with shards of paper. "Too bad this isn't a receipt or something. But that would be too easy, wouldn't it?" She examined the corners of paper closely, but didn't seem to draw any better conclusions than he had. "Looks like junk mail," she said with a sigh.

"That's what I thought, too."

He went to take the bag from her, but she tugged it back. "Wait. I think—I think I can make out part of a name." She shook the bag, attempting to bring the piece that'd caught her attention clear of the others. "Some letters are missing off the beginning and end, but I swear it spells out a very familiar name." She looked straight at him, sending his pulse racing. "Henry Davenport."

Chapter Nine

Laurel

Laurel had pushed the idea to have Ava's birthday cookout at Chase's house, mostly because she thought it was a shame for such a lovely firepit area to remain empty night after night. They couldn't light a fire, not until Sunset Ridge got some very badly needed rain, and maybe not even then, but it was a great gathering space. A vision of hers Chase had brought to life in her absence. It was hard for that *not* to touch her heart.

"I can't believe you talked me into this." Chase carried an empty plate in from the grill and rinsed it off in the sink.

"I didn't. Your sister did."

"And who convinced *her*?"

Their easy banter was growing more dangerous with each passing day, but Laurel's guard had begun to collapse, and that could be blamed almost entirely on their explosive kiss. Memories of it drew her gaze even now to the second-floor staircase. "You never did tell me about your renovation project upstairs."

"I haven't really gotten a good start on it. Not with this case chewing up so much time and energy."

"Talk to Henry yet?"

"Not yet. Planning to do that tomorrow. Only want to bother him once for questioning so I don't get reprimanded for that too."

Sensing discussing the case was only going to work Chase up, Laurel switched tactics. "What's your plan with the upstairs?"

Chase searched a cupboard, his arm disappearing up to his elbow as he reached in for a bottle of seasoning. "Thought I'd make those two smallest bedrooms one larger guest suite."

Laurel immediately warmed to the idea. "Like a place where your parents can stay when they visit."

"Yeah, exactly." Their gaze met, and Laurel found herself trapped by it so long her heart fluttered erratically. The same way it had when they first started dating.

She forced her attention to the macaroni salad, stirring it despite that it was already well-mixed. "How are your parents? They're in Minnesota, right?"

She felt the heat of him as he hovered beside her, and gulped a swallow. With Chase this close, all she could think about was kissing him again. But another kiss would be selfish on her part. She hadn't changed her mind about the papers. "You know how they are," he said in a low voice that tickled her ear and sent shivers throughout her chest.

"Chase—"

"Knock, knock!" Ava's lyrical greeting rang through the house, causing Zeus to bark in excitement as he rushed to the door. Ava didn't wait to be let in this time.

Chase stared at Laurel a beat longer, dropping his gaze to her lips, no doubt on purpose. He was making this *so* hard. Which was why Laurel vowed to tell him the one painful truth she'd kept under lock and key after the party ended. Tonight.

"You weren't supposed to bring anything," Laurel scolded at the sight of Ava carrying a stack of bowls.

"I'm the birthday girl," Ava insisted, setting three covered containers of various colors on the counter beside Laurel's macaroni salad. A fourth she stuck in the fridge. "I can do what I want."

"I tried to stop her," Brayden, Ava's fiancé, said with a helpless shrug as he and their golden retriever, Elsie, followed. The two dogs sniffed in greeting, tails winding slowly until they were wagging excitedly. Chase opened the sliding door and both pups zoomed outside. "But you know Ava. When she has her mind set to something—"

Ava cut him off with an enthusiastic kiss that made Laurel jealous. She missed that feeling of being completely immersed in someone. Totally and undeniably in love. So ridiculously happy the negativity of the world couldn't penetrate such a strong shield.

Laurel'd never felt with another man the way she'd felt with Chase. She doubted she ever would again. The idea of these birthday gatherings—one or both of them bringing someone else—ripped at her heart.

"Why don't you go help Chase with the grill?" Ava suggested when the two finally came up for air. Turning to Laurel, Ava looped her arm through hers and dragged her toward the living room. "I need to talk to Laurel. It's really girly stuff. You guys'll just be bored."

"Am I in trouble?" Laurel asked with a half-hearted laugh, hoping to cover up her anxiousness once they were alone.

"Of course not, silly." Ava pulled her down onto the L-shaped sofa. The dark grey one she'd picked out with Chase when they first moved in that was now half covered in throw blankets, no doubt to catch most of the dog hair. She could picture Zeus being a couch-hog. "I just wanted to talk to you about something before everyone got here so it could be a private conversation."

Ava slipped her tote-sized purse off her shoulder and fished out a pamphlet, but when Laurel went to take it, Ava held on so tightly Laurel feared it would rip. "What is this?"

"Before I tell you, promise me you'll keep an open mind. And you're not allowed to get mad. It's my birthday, and I won't allow it."

"You would pull that card."

"Humor me."

Laurel turned her attention toward the kitchen, unsure whether she wanted Chase's interruption or not. Whatever Ava had to show her felt serious. She was enjoying lighthearted fantasy over grave realities right now. But considering she was boxed in on the couch, she relented. "Fine, I promise."

"My mom has a friend who is pretty high up the chain at an adoption agency." Ava bit down on her bottom lip, watching Laurel, but giving her a few seconds to process. Desperately needed seconds, because her stomach dropped and tied in knots all at once. Laurel's entire body felt ten degrees warmer. "I just want you to *think* about it, Laurel. There's absolutely no pressure. It's just, don't you think it's crazy how you missed a signature and it took someone five years to find it? That sort of thing doesn't happen in real life. That should've been caught within days of Jenkins submitting the paperwork. Your still being married to my brother isn't some fluke. It's fate, and you know it."

Sweat beaded Laurel's brow. Her throat was swollen shut, her words lodged there. All she could do was shake her head.

Ava cupped both Laurel's hands in hers, her eyes gentle. "I won't tell you what to do. I just wanted you to consider another option. Maybe you already have at one time, but think about it again. My mom's friend can help cut through some red tape and speed up the process, but it's a favor that can only be asked once. I'm guessing you've never discussed this idea with Chase, considering. Before you sign—"

"Thank you." Laurel snagged the pamphlet from Ava but refused to look at it. She'd promised not to get upset, and she was going to keep that promise. But adoption was something she'd already considered and dismissed. It didn't feel *right*. "I need some time," she said carefully, biting back the words urging to escape but would only leave them fighting.

"I know. This isn't something you have to figure out tonight."

The doorbell saved Laurel from a complete meltdown. As Kinley, Ryder, and Rowdy charged inside, she slipped into the master bedroom and closed the door behind her. She needed a moment to catch her breath and ward off tears. *So many tears this week!* She wasn't prepared for the overwhelming scent of Chase lingering in the air. One of cologne, smoky grill, and rugged outdoorsmen. She inhaled it, and it helped her find her calm center.

She shoved the pamphlet beneath a stack of books on the dresser. "I'll come back for you later," she told the folded glossy paper. Compartmentalizing her emotions, she breathed deep. Several minutes later, she felt composed and reached for the doorknob. But the door opened first, causing her to hop back in surprise with a squeak.

"What are you doing in here?" Chase's eyebrow rose playfully.

"Got lost."

He laughed, closing the door behind them. "Sure you did, Laurel." When he drew her into his arms, she was helpless to fight it. The pull between them was stronger than any tide. She welcomed his kiss, drawing him down to her with both hands on his neck. Kissing Chase meant she didn't have to think about anything too serious. Thinking about *anything* while his lips made her toes curl and butterflies erupt in her tummy was impossible anyway.

"Wow," Chase said when he finally let her come up for air. "Try to tell me you don't want to stay married after *that*."

Her gaze flashed to the stack of books, then to the door. "I-I shouldn't have done that."

"Liar." He kissed her again, just to prove his point. Darn it if she didn't melt into him a second time.

Faintly, she recalled they had friends in the backyard. Something about a birthday. It wasn't until she heard a chorus of barking dogs that she was able to push her palm flat against his chest and create space between them. "We need to get back to the party." She hated that her words were breathless and her fingertips tingling. She really missed being his wife, but that secret was hers alone to keep.

"After you."

With a deep breath, Laurel emerged from the bedroom feeling as if she'd been doing something inappropriate. Never mind that they'd only been kissing and they were technically still *married*. A smile tugged at her lips, and she gave up fighting it.

"There you two are," Kinley said the second they stepped through the sliding-glass door and onto the deck. Zeus zipped up to her long enough for a quick head scratch, then darted after Rowdy. Elsie, the older golden retriever, watched the pair from the deck, heavily panting as if she'd had enough of play time.

Everything about this moment—the dogs playing, their friends gathered in couples around the deck, music softly playing, the aroma of burgers cooking on the grill—felt blissfully normal. This was what Laurel always imagined it would be like, except with some rug rats running around the backyard by now. With both her best friends getting married in less than two months, they'd be starting on their families soon, she suspected.

Ava's gaze flickered to hers, a gentle smile sent her way. *Adoption.* Laurel wanted to believe it was the answer to all her prayers, but it still didn't feel right. It didn't feel right to rob Chase of his chance to have biological children when he still could.

"The burgers are ready," Brayden called over his shoulder as he shoveled them into a heap on a plate.

Chase dropped his hand on her shoulder, startling her from her thoughts. "Smile. It's a party, Laurel."

"Let's eat!" Ava announced. "Then we're playing yard games."

A couple of groans erupted.

"It's *my* birthday," she reminded them.

"On *my* birthday, you're all going fishing in *my* boat," Ryder declared. "Even if it's raining."

When Chase slipped back inside, Kinley popped to Laurel's side. "You should see the cake I got her," she said proudly. "It was all I could do not to eat it myself. Bonita outdid herself."

Channeling a skill she had mastered well over the past five years, Laurel pushed her negative emotions—the sadness, anxiousness, and dread—into an imaginary box and closed the lid. There was plenty of time to face the hard truths before Jenkins returned. Tonight, she wanted to enjoy this blessedly perfect evening with her best friends.

Hours passed in a blink. The group had relocated to the firepit area, and Chase even poked at the pit as if there were a fire. She kept sneaking glances at him, wondering if he'd been able to forget about the case long enough to enjoy the evening. Mostly, she thought yes. But every once in a while, she caught a flicker of something in his eyes that made her think otherwise.

Laurel emptied her diet soda and stood. "Anyone need something to drink while I'm going in?" She took a couple of requests and slipped into the mostly dark kitchen. The overcast sky made the Alaskan summer night duskier than usual, teasing at rain they needed but would not get.

Out of habit, Laurel started to clean up the counters. Covering the macaroni salad and sticking it in the fridge, closing chip and hamburger bun bags, filling a trash bag and tying it shut.

"You get lost again?" Chase teased, the door sliding closed behind him. "Our friends are thirsty."

"The macaroni salad was still out," she answered, as if that explained everything.

He closed the distance between them, making her regret leaving the light off. It wasn't that she didn't want to kiss him again, because that's all she'd been thinking the whole evening. Chase was the only man who'd ever made her body tingle from a single graze of his lips. *Adoption.* That word rang in her head again. *Maybe . . .*

"Laurel, you have that troubled look in your eyes again. What is it?"

She glanced out the window, watching her friends laugh and toss the ball around for the only dog not completely worn out—Zeus. They didn't seem put out by the absence of their hosts. She could tell him now, while she was as close to brave as she was going to get about this.

"There's something I never told you."

Chase tucked her loose blonde curls behind her ear, his fingertips blazing a trail across her cheek. "Another secret?"

"Yeah." *Just spit it out, Laurel. It's not going to get any easier.* "I can't have—"

Chase's radio blared from the counter with its familiar emergency tone. He grabbed the radio and waited for the message from the dispatcher. Ryder was inside half a second before she spoke. *Fire and rescue needed immediately at 459 Choke Cherry Lane. Structure fire and at least one known injury.* The rest of the message was a blur to Laurel as the men urgently rushed about. The three darted out the door together, heading to the fire hall and leaving the women and dogs gathered in the kitchen.

Ava popped the lid off the half-eaten sheet cake, picking up a fork and diving in. "They're going to be a while," she said casually, as if she weren't the least bit worried about her brother or fiancé heading out to the second fire in less than a week.

Kinley handed Laurel a plastic fork. "I'm sure it'll be fine. They'll have the fire trucks out there in minutes since it's in town. Fire will be out in no time."

Laurel wanted to feel comfort in that thought, but two fires in one week in Sunset Ridge felt ominous. She couldn't help but wonder if they were related, which only made her wonder if she was turning into some sort of conspiracy theorist. *459 Choke Cherry Lane.* She picked up her phone and pulled up her map app.

"That's a couple blocks from your parents' place, right?" Kinley asked between bites of cakes.

"Yeah." From the map app, she couldn't be

certain. But she thought the address was awfully close to the Davenport residence. She considered going home, watching the events from the hill her parents' house sat on. But one look at Zeus and she decided she couldn't abandon him. Despite all the warning bells going off in her head, tonight she'd stay until Chase came home.

Chapter Ten

CHASE

Chase stood on the curb with folded arms and studied the scene. Hours later, the fire threat was eliminated and all surrounding homes, outbuildings, and trees were safe from going up in flames. But the usual relief he felt once a fire was out didn't come, and in its place was suspicion. Everyone else was labeling this fire a coincidence. 'Lucky' was also a word he'd heard tossed around because the flames were centrally located in the detached garage and never spread to the house or any neighboring properties.

That it was the Davenports' detached garage that

accidentally went up in flames didn't have anyone batting an eye, aside from a few gossipy neighbors and the newspaper report Glenn kept chasing away.

To Chase, though, everything about this situation reeked of ill intentions.

"You've got that serious, sour look on your face," Chief Bauer said, joining him on the street while the rest of the crew searched for the last embers. "Please tell me you're not convinced Henry has enemies. I don't need another conspiracy theory floating around. Evelynn Marsh will eat that right up and get the whole town in a tizzy. It was hard enough to convince her to go home tonight. This was an accident, nothing more."

Had it not been for Laurel's sharp eye, he might've agreed with that theory. But the scrap of mail in the fire—the one with most of Henry Davenport's name—unsettled him. Though it seemed like a stretch, there was the thought that he might've set a fire *in* town to make it look as though they were being targeted. No one with half a brain would try something so stupid during a burn ban. Henry was a lifelong Alaskan well aware of that risk in a dry spell.

A few minutes later, half the block could've been up in flames.

"You believe their story, then?" Chase asked,

failing to hide the exasperation in his tone. If he wasn't careful, Glenn would insist on taking over this investigation. It would be written off before anyone second-guessed it. Keeping his mouth shut might be the only thing that gave him a chance to dig into this the right way.

"What's not to believe? Henry forgot to turn the kerosene heater off in the garage. It caught fire. Ever see the inside of his garage? He's not exactly a tidy guy."

More kerosene. Chase kept that thought to himself, no longer sure who he could trust to have his back on this. That any evidence to dispute an accidental fire was as scarce at this scene as the last didn't help his case, either.

A curious neighbor waved Glenn over, but before he trotted off, he turned to Chase. "See that this report is turned in with the other one Monday." He didn't wait for so much as a nod of confirmation before he turned his back and hurried across the street.

Chase spotted Ryder in the Davenports' driveway, still dressed in jeans and a Cabela's T-shirt from their earlier cookout, talking to both Henry and Crissy. Chase hoped he was asking the right questions, but the only way to know for certain was to join them. Before he could close the distance however, someone else stepped into his way.

"Fancy meeting you here." Tuck Granger's voice grated against Chase's ears. He was surprised the man was still in town, since the only thing he was waiting on could easily be sent to him in an email. He trusted the man about as much as he trusted a hungry grizzly bear.

"Thought you'd be in Anchorage by now."

"I like it here. It's a nice break from the wife. You know how it goes." That cackle made Chase want to punch the man, the ugly impulse urging him to get away. Rarely did anyone draw out that impulse, and it unsettled him. The best thing to do was walk away before Ryder was forced to arrest him.

Before Chase could escape, Tuck added, "Say, Deputy Chief Monroe, you finish up that report yet? My boss is hounding me hourly about collecting it."

Chase stared straight at Tuck, studying his expression hard. He had a string of questions he wanted to fire at the man, but he'd never been formally trained in interrogation. Anything he now might work against him. Especially with that urge to deck the guy growing stronger.

"Monday," he answered curtly before he marched off toward the site where the garage once stood, needing to cool off before he approached the Davenports. A melted snow machine, remnants of the heater, and several dozen random tools littered the ground where the garage stood only hours before.

"You good, man?" Marc asked, wiping sweat from his brow. Now that the fire was out, the men had ditched their helmets and opened their turnout coats. Chase had to look twice to be sure it was Laurel's brother, because they hardly spoke a word to each other unless forced. "You look like you want to slug someone."

"I do."

"Well, don't. You're not my favorite person, but it's not worth it."

"I won't." Chase let out an aggravated sigh. "Just don't like how this smells, that's all."

"The melted plastic or the pile-of-crap story those two are telling?" Marc said with a nod at the Davenports, surprising Chase. Even his best friend thought he was trying to shove puzzle pieces together that didn't fit.

"Both."

Chase watched the couple talking to Ryder, their expressions illuminated by the orange glow of a streetlight. In his ash-stained sweatpants and dirty T-shirt, Henry was either a really good actor, or genuinely perplexed. Maybe Glenn was right. Maybe Henry forgot to turn off the heater and was embarrassed by his carelessness.

"Don't get strong-armed into doing something that doesn't feel right," Marc added, nodding at him before he returned to clean-up. It was a relief to have an ally in the department, even if they were enemies outside of it.

Chase helped the crew until there was nothing more for them to do, biding his time until Chief Bauer left. Ryder was more likely to let Chase get in a few casual questions with Henry before he stopped him. Glenn would keep him from spitting out a single one. He waited until the fire truck headed down the street and pushed his luck.

"Glad you folks are okay," he said to both Davenports. "This could've gotten ugly really quick."

"I swear I don't remember even *using* that heater tonight." Henry looked at Chase, a plea to believe him in his desperate eyes. Oddly enough, Chase did. If there was a culprit in all of this, he doubted Henry was the guilty one.

"You've been very forgetful lately," Crissy snapped. "I've had to turn that heater off half a dozen times this year because he forgot. We're just lucky it didn't burn down sooner." Looking at Chase, she added, "It was an accident, that's all. Don't go believing we have enemies out to get us or anything crazy like that. We don't. I'm going to bed, gentlemen."

Watching Crissy spin on her heel and march toward her house reminded Chase how late it was. *Just past midnight.* Was it coincidence that these fires happened in the evenings? If they were truly caused by a cold squatter and a forgetful man working on a project in a chilled garage, then no. But if it were someone trying to set a fire and stand a better chance at not being seen, they'd use the cover of the dusky darkness to help cloak them.

"What were you working on?" Chase asked Henry before the man could turn to leave.

"Building a spice rack. Crissy's been bugging me all week to do it." He shook his head. "It wasn't that cold tonight. I really don't think I even used the heater. But she's not wrong. I have been forgetting things lately. Where I put my wallet or car key . . . found them in the freezer yesterday. You believe that?"

"It was just an accident," Ryder reassured Henry at the same time he directed a quick warning glare to

150

Chase to back off. It was obvious that Henry was rattled by not only the fires, but the possibility of losing his mind. He didn't look like a guilty man, which unraveled Chase's theory.

Chase pressed his luck with one more question. "That night the cabin on Jack Rabbit Creek Road went up in flames, you were out that way." He ignored Ryder's stern look to drop it. It was the one question that had plagued him the most. "Why?"

"Just needed a quiet place to think." Henry shrugged pitifully. "Crissy thinks I need to be on medication on account of my forgetting things. As if I'm some old geezer. I'm only forty-nine, for crying out loud. I went out there to think it through. I hate doctors, and I'm not convinced I'm as forgetful as she thinks." He looked back over his shoulder at his house. "Can I go inside?"

"Yes. We'll meet at the station tomorrow to knock out the paperwork," Ryder told him.

Chase waited until Henry was to his door before he spoke. "You really think he forgot he turned on a heater?"

"I believe *he* thinks he didn't."

It was too much to hope that Ryder would take his side on this. "Ever find out that amount?" Chase asked, watching Granger poking his nose around the spot where the garage once stood. He wished he could wrap up his report if for no other reason than to get the adjuster out of town.

"No."

Chase swallowed his frustration, biting back words because too many people still loitered around them. "I'd really like to have that figure by Monday."

"Me, too." Ryder scrubbed a hand over his hair and down his neck, fighting a yawn. "Been trying to call the insurance company since you asked. Granger's based out of the Anchorage office, but no one wants to answer the phone or return my calls. Before you ask, yes, I've tried to reach the main office, but they just give me the runaround and tell me I need to talk to the Anchorage office."

"You don't think that's strange?"

"No, not really." With another yawn, Ryder eyed his truck. "Ever been on the phone with an insurance company? It's a pain in the you-know-what to get information out of them." As the last fire department vehicle departed the scene, Ryder added, "C'mon, it's late. I'll give you a ride home."

"Thanks. Zeus is probably pacing circles at the front window, tearing up one of my favorite socks." Nights like tonight, it really stunk that Laurel wasn't at home waiting for him. He wanted his wife in his life permanently, and he was running out of time to make it happen. Sure, they could work things out down the road even with the divorce final, but a gut feeling told him that was doubtful.

"I'm canceling my fishing trip," Ryder grumbled. "Kinley thinks I should stick around this weekend in case you need my help. *And* to keep you out of trouble. Starting with no more unsolicited questions. I don't know if you could tell, but Henry's truly rattled by all this. The last thing he needs is you cooking up conspiracy theories you can't back up with evidence. You'll have the whole town pitted against him if you're not careful."

Ryder was only doing his job, as Chase was, so he didn't argue.

"I'll help put all this to bed if you want," Ryder added. "But you owe me. When this is all over, you're taking the boat out with me, wife or no wife. We're getting those kings before they leave."

"Deal."

When Ryder pulled into Chase's driveway, he was surprised to see the glow of a living room lamp. That Laurel had left a light on for Zeus made him swear he was falling more deeply in love with her every day. The thought made him wonder what she'd been about to tell him in the kitchen before the call came in.

Whatever it was, it was one of her biggest secrets.

"Chase?"

"Yeah?"

"Don't make me arrest you, okay?" With those ominous words, Ryder backed up and drove away.

Chase unlocked the front door, surprised when Zeus didn't immediately bombard him at the door. Even groggy, he was always excited for Chase to come home on a late night. He'd barely hung up his jacket when he spotted the dog on the couch, curled up next to a blanket-covered heap.

Laurel.

His chest warmed at the sight of her sleeping, Zeus curled protectively against her. He didn't dare wake her. As he crept from the front door toward the master bedroom, the pup lifted his head. His tail thumped a few times as if to say hello, then settled.

Chase nodded, not a bit disappointed that Zeus chose Laurel over him tonight.

After a long hot shower, he snuck into the kitchen and ate a cold burger. Part of him hoped Laurel would wake up. He craved her company, her reassuring words that he wasn't losing his marbles over these fires. But because he didn't want her to leave, he settled simply for having her here, in the house she belonged in.

He pulled the blanket over her shoulders, scratched a sleepy Zeus behind the ears, and went to bed.

Chapter Eleven

Laurel

Sunlight beamed Laurel in the face until she forced her eyes open. The room was much too bright to be her basement bedroom pointed toward the west. The aroma of bacon tickled her senses. *Odd.* Stretching her legs, one fell off the edge of the bed and the other bumped into— *I'm on a couch?*

The events of last night returned to Laurel in a rush. Standing with Chase in the dim kitchen, about to confess her biggest secret. The fire call coming in. Eating enough leftover birthday cake to lull her into a sugar coma. Her decision to stay with Zeus after Ava and Kinley called it a night. The dog curling up beside her on the couch. She expected to wake up when Chase got home and leave. That's what she'd texted Haylee.

She dared to sit up, searching for her phone, and was greeted seconds later by an excitable wet nose from the pup who'd kept her company all night. "Hey, buddy."

"Making bacon, eggs over easy, and toast," Chase announced from the kitchen. "It'll be ready in about two minutes."

Laurel definitely shouldn't stay for breakfast, but her stomach growled in objection at the thought of leaving. "I didn't hear you come in last night," she called back, lifting the blanket and throw pillows to find her phone. "How late were you at the fire?"

"Almost one."

Shoving her hand behind the cushions, she came up with both her phone and a bone-shaped treat. Zeus must've spotted it immediately, because he plopped his bottom down so hard the area rug shimmied beneath him. She tossed him the treat and forced her stiff legs to stretch into standing. "Fifteen messages?" she mumbled.

"What's that?"

"Nothing." She skimmed the string of texts from Ava and Kinley—both confirming lunch plans today to discuss wedding details, one from Mom asking her to pick up some diapers, and the rest from Haylee demanding to know why she was still gone. One early morning message suggested Laurel had decided to stay married and already moved out. Haylee could be almost as dramatic as their other sister when she was running on little to no sleep. She didn't bother to read the rest.

"Orange juice or coffee?" Chase asked as he slid a plate in front of Laurel at the breakfast bar.

She set her phone off to the side, leaving it on silent. She'd respond to everyone after she shook away the grogginess. "Coffee. Please, coffee. Just bring me the pot."

"You didn't sleep *that* bad, did you? That couch is crazy comfortable."

Her back didn't ache and she didn't remember waking up even once after falling asleep. "The couch was great. I think it's just life that has me a little out of sorts." She offered him a reassuring smile, then switched the subject. "What happened last night?"

"Davenports lost their detached garage."

"The Davenports?"

"What a coincidence, huh?"

She accepted the oversized mug, already fixed

with creamer and sugar, and sipped eagerly. "Let me guess. It looks like an accident too?"

"Kerosene heater didn't get turned off, or so Crissy is saying. Henry was in there, making a spice rack, but swears he didn't even use it." Chase carried his own plate to the spot beside her and sat down. Though he seemed to treat it as the most normal thing in the world, Laurel's heart pounded at his proximity. A hint of his enticing cologne drifted to her, and it made her yearn to wrap herself in his arms like they had so many sunny mornings like this when they were first married.

"So the heater caused the fire?"

"Yeah, the evidence agrees with that much." Chase ate a strip of bacon, swallowed, and added, "Guess who else showed up at the scene last night?"

"Who?"

"Mr. Insurance Adjuster."

Laurel dropped the piece of buttered toast that had been halfway to her mouth. "Why is he even still here?"

"Same question I asked him." Chase's easy-going demeanor switched to cool in a flash. "Laurel, there's something about that guy that just rubs me wrong. I just can't put my finger on any of it."

"You don't think he's a part of this?"

"It doesn't make sense. I mean, what would he benefit?" Chase turned his gaze over his shoulder, peering at her. Laurel's whole body tingled at that one look, making her forget that five years had ever passed with them apart. "Now Bauer wants me to get *both* reports done on Monday."

Monday. The same day she was supposed to seal their fate. "Chase, I—"

"Your phone is lighting up like a New Year's Eve fireworks display," he said with a nod. "Do you need to get that?"

Ava and Kinley had added Laurel to a group text about the lunch date. Today they were trying to finalize flowers. Laurel couldn't believe how much work that one simple task was already turning out to be, and they hadn't even gotten started. "I have to meet the girls for more wedding plans." Her face dropped when she looked down at her clothes. "I can't go out like this. I can't even go *home* like this."

"Take a shower here," Chase suggested.

"And put on yesterday's clothes? No thanks." Somehow she'd have to sneak back into her parents' house and change so Mom wouldn't know she'd been out all night. Never mind that she had a perfectly rational explanation. Mom would blow it out of proportion. "And I'm not borrowing any of your clothes," she added before he could offer. "That would be harder to explain."

"How scandalous that my *wife* spent the night," he teased before draining his glass of orange juice. "You have clothes here, in those boxes you still need to go through."

"Oh." How many outfits had she left hanging in the closet after shoving her whole life into two suitcases? Her chest constricted at the thought of going through boxes that would no doubt sway her decision to sign the papers. This was how it had to be. She loved Chase more than she would ever love anyone, and that was why she had to force him to move on. To find someone who could give him what she never could.

"At least half of the boxes are clothes," he said, carrying his empty plate to the sink. He called Zeus to the back door. "Grab a shower."

"Hey," she said before he could follow the dog into the backyard. "Who got hurt?"

"What's that?"

"On the call, the dispatcher said there was one known injury. Who was it?"

"Arnie Power. He tried to put out the fire with an extinguisher before we showed up. Some flames got his arm and gave him second-degree burns. Before they took him to the hospital, he was already bragging about battle scars."

Laurel laughed softly. "I'm glad he's okay."

"Me, too."

"Do you think he saw anything?"

"I'll check with Ryder. Good thinking."

They shared an easy smile, one that made her forget this wasn't normal. "I better grab that shower."

The shower was the easy part, even if she did end up smelling like Chase's body wash. The boxes were another story. She dressed in the first acceptable outfit she could find and closed the box back up. If stupid clothes could make her tear up, what would the rest of the contents do to her?

She peeked out the kitchen window, watching Chase toss a ball to Zeus. The dog had masses of energy. It amazed her that he could sprint like a rocket and still spend all night cuddled up with her on the couch, hardly moving a muscle. He was the perfect dog. The one they'd always wanted to find. *Keep Chase happy, buddy.*

While the two continued to play outside, Laurel carried the boxes one and two at a time to her car parked half a block down the street. She'd stayed out of the driveway last night to give everyone else decent parking. But she didn't mind the exercise now, and welcomed the way it sharpened her resolve.

When the dining room was empty of her stuff, she took the stairs two at a time. She didn't want to alert Chase. He would offer to help or insist she come back another time to go through it here. And she'd let him talk her into it. If there were any other boxes of her things, she'd find them on her own.

The first door on the left was open again. The same door Chase had caught her about to open the other evening and distracted her with wonderful, breath-stealing kisses. He'd saved her from facing the pain. It didn't matter if the walls were still the same soft yellow or if he'd converted it into an office. She would still see a nursery.

With a deep breath, she pushed it open and gasped.

A beautiful cedar log crib stood directly across from the open door, near the main window. Chase had found the design online after they found out they were pregnant and been determined he would build one like it. One they would use not only for their first, but all of their kids to follow. She never imagined he would carry through with the project after they lost the baby. Tears stung her eyes as she ran her fingers along the smooth wood. Had he built it because he wanted to try again?

Laurel couldn't breathe.

She shouldn't be in here.

Backpedaling to the door, she ran squarely into Chase's chest. "Hey," he said, turning her into his arms and brushing away her tears. "I didn't want you to see it this way. I'm sorry, sweetheart."

She wanted to give in and cry while he held her. In his embrace it was impossible to feel alone. But that desire was completely selfish. She pushed her palm flat against his chest, but he didn't loosen his hold. "I have to go."

"Laurel—"

"Please, let me go." She wriggled free and hurried down the steps, grabbing her phone on the way out the door. Her heart nearly cracked in two when she spotted Zeus staring in the window after her.

Chapter Twelve

CHASE

Chase entered the grocery store, on the hunt for both a bottle of wine to bring to dinner and the biggest bag of frosted animal cookies he could find for Haylee. He doubted any other Evans knew he'd been invited to their Sunday family dinner, but hopefully the wine would keep him from getting kicked out the second he showed up.

After Laurel left him standing in the doorway yesterday, Chase felt defeated. He was certain that her finding the crib on her own had demolished his chances of convincing her to stay married, especially since she sent his calls straight to voicemail and ignored his texts. But that afternoon, he received an Instagram message from Haylee, and his hope renewed.

She promised she had a plan, and he needed to be there for it to work.

Tonight was his last chance to change Laurel's mind.

He spent an excessive amount of time debating the wine choice. Laurel had always handled that, leaving him to scour the shelves for vaguely familiar labels and hoping he didn't mess it up. Because he couldn't decide between a white or red, he grabbed one of each. Whether or not they were decent selections would soon be determined.

His phone buzzed in his pocket as he exited the store, which was why he didn't see the woman he crashed into until it was too late. He recovered his briefly airborne cell as her purse slid off her arm and thudded against the pavement, some of the contents spilling out.

In a miraculous but awkward ninja maneuver, he kept hold of the wine bottles. Haylee's cookies might be more crushed than she was used to, but it was better than a wet bag full of broken glass. "I'm so sorry—" Only now did Chase see who it was. "Mrs. Davenport, I apologize. I wasn't watching—"

"Crissy. My name's Crissy. I hate being called *Mrs. Davenport*. I'm only thirty-six, you know. Way too young to feel like some old crone." Her words spilled out quickly with exasperation as she crouched to gather the scattered contents. "Don't suppose you finished that report?"

Chase spotted a small tube rolling down the sidewalk and hurried after it. "I'll have them done soon," he answered, stopping the runaway canister with his foot. He refused to promise tomorrow to anyone, even the chief. If he could buy a couple more days, he could solve this the right way. He crouched down to pick up the tube and nearly dropped the grocery bag. It was a black lipstick case with the same crocodile patterns and double heart emblem etched into the silver strip.

"Can I have that back?" Crissy held out an open palm impatiently.

As Chase handed it over, most of the missing pieces seemed to fall into place. Henry hadn't started the fires. *Crissy* had. But his only chance to prove it was now tucked into her purse. He couldn't go to the chief and demand they search Crissy's purse. Even if they could, the coincidence would mean nothing to them. It wasn't evidence enough to prove her guilt.

"Your insurance adjuster head back to Anchorage yet?"

Crissy raised an eyebrow at him, but only briefly. "He decided to stick around after Friday night. Says he'll be on his way after you finish the investigation reports. Can't imagine what's taking you so long. Heard they caught the hitchhiker near Girdwood. I already told Ryder we don't want to press charges or anything. An accident is an accident."

"Just being thorough," Chase said. "Have a nice day, Crissy."

"Chase?"

He stopped at the front of his truck and turned back. "Yeah?"

"If you have any more questions, come to me. Henry's mind is slipping. After these fires, it just seems to be getting worse. I think it's an early onset of Alzheimer's."

Not a chance he believed her, but he gave her a nod and hopped in his truck.

Chase's first impulse was to call Laurel about the lipstick. Had it not been for her, he never would've paid such careful attention. He would've handed the lipstick tube back to Crissy and never made the connection. Because of Laurel, he was ninety-five percent certain that Crissy started the fires to collect the insurance money.

Instead of Laurel, he called Ryder.

"I don't have the dollar amount yet," Ryder said before Chase could get in a word. "I'll get it tomorrow, even if I have to have Liam fly me up to Anchorage. Happy?"

"I think I know who's responsible. Crissy—"

"Stop right there." Ryder let out a loud sigh that sounded like a gust of wind through the phone. "Chase, you know I'll always have your back, right? Which means if I think you're overstaying your welcome in conspiracy-ville, I'm going to tell you."

"You think I'm wrong."

"I think you're not thinking straight because of this whole deal with Laurel."

If he and Ryder hadn't been best friends for the better part of two decades, he might think Ryder was in on this whole thing. But that theory *did* make him sound as if he'd booked a one-way ticket to conspiracy-ville. "Just do me a favor?" Chase relented. "Find out the number tomorrow before I have to sign off on those reports?"

"I've been calling three times a day."

Odd, considering Granger claimed his boss was bothering him constantly. Chase almost said as much, but he didn't want to give Ryder yet another reason to think he'd lost his marbles. In a way, he thought he understood what Henry was going through. "I'll touch base with you tomorrow."

"Stay out of trouble, okay?"

Ending the call, Chase headed across town to the Evans' residence.

Stomach in knots, he parked along the street and made the long, steep walk up their driveway. The *log mansion*, as many called it, was one of the biggest homes in town. One Laurel's family had owned for three decades or more. There were enough bedrooms for all the Evans siblings to visit and not share a room or need a couch. They'd spent the first couple weeks after their honeymoon in that house while they waited on their own to close. He missed the days when he was openly accepted as one of the family.

His last Sunday family dinner here had been more than five years ago. They'd been ridiculously excited about the baby, the puppy they were going to adopt, and the nursery they had just painted. Twice Laurel almost slipped and made the announcement early, but they'd agreed to wait until the second trimester.

Little did they know their child would never make it that far along.

Ignoring the impulse to turn heel and run, Chase knocked on the door, hoping either Haylee or Cody would answer the door.

But it was Marc.

"What are you doing here?" Marc growled at him, their brief alliance from the night of the fire already up in smoke.

"Is that Chase?" Haylee's voice called before she wedged her way between Marc and the door. "Hey, you made it!" She pushed the door open as she shoved Marc back with her petite frame. "Marc, *I* invited him."

"Why?"

"Knock it off," Haylee snapped at him, her narrowed glare successfully chasing off her oldest brother. "Sorry about that. I didn't tell anyone you were coming. Didn't want to scare off *you know who*. Plan can't work if she isn't here."

"What is the plan, exactly?" With Marc no longer blocking the door with his linebacker frame, Chase was able to scan the chaos inside. Beth held her granddaughter on one hip as she carried a breadbasket to the table, shouting at Cody to grab the plates and silverware. Jerry sat in his favorite recliner, head ducked behind the paper as long as he could get away with it. *Some things never change.*

"You'll just have to trust me."

Another scan, and he still didn't find Laurel.

"She's downstairs," Haylee said, tugging Chase inside. "C'mon."

"Chase," Beth said, finally seeing him. "What a surprise."

"Mom, I invited him, okay? Everyone needs to be nice."

Beth's concerned expression at that tidbit forced Chase to clear the air. The last thing he needed was any of the Evans who already considered him the bad guy to think he was preying on the youngest sister. "I'm still in love with Laurel, just to be clear." He held out the bag to Haylee. "I brought some wine."

"And my cookies! You're the best, Chase." She carried the bag into the kitchen, leaving him with Beth and Melly.

"I haven't met you before," he said to the precious little girl staring at him with fascinated wide blue eyes. "She's absolutely breathtaking."

"You say that because she's quiet right now, but don't let her fool you into thinking she's a demure little thing," Beth said with a laugh before turning on her baby voice. "But yes, you are a little angel even when you're screaming bloody murder, aren't you?"

"A month old today, I hear."

"Growing up so fast." When the oven timer sounded, Beth held Melly out to him. "Can you take her? I need to get the scalloped potatoes before they burn." She didn't leave him much choice, but Chase didn't mind. He loved kids, and most of them loved him. Maybe if Laurel saw him holding her niece, it would remind her of what they could try again to have. Was that Haylee's plan?

As everyone bustled around him, some oblivious to his presence, others noticeably irritated, Chase carried Melly to the window and quietly pointed out the world to her. She didn't follow his finger, but instead stared up at him in wonder with those big blue eyes. "You're going to break a lot of hearts, aren't you, Melly?"

"What are you doing here?" Laurel's voice caused his pulse to double, then triple. He wasn't certain ambushing her like this was wise, but he was putting his trust in her youngest sister. Haylee had assured him that this was the last ace up his sleeve. He sincerely hoped she was right.

LAUREL

. . .

"I invited him," Haylee said from behind Laurel's shoulder.

Finding Chase in their house holding her niece at the window, looking happy and so natural, made her heart ache. Painfully reminding her once again why she had to sign those papers tomorrow. *One more day*. Why couldn't she stay away from him for one more flipping day?

"I didn't know you two were friends," Laurel said between gritted teeth, more confused than ever. Hadn't Haylee been the one over-the-top upset about the idea of Laurel getting back together with him and moving out?

"We follow each other on Instagram."

"Since when?" Laurel demanded.

"Since forever." Haylee rolled her eyes. "You should try *reading* the texts I sent you." Haylee patted her on the shoulder before she wove between them to take Melly. "Let's get you fed, baby girl, before you decide to have a meltdown at the dinner table and scare away our poor guest."

As much as she was annoyed with her sister for putting her in this super awkward position, she didn't want Haylee to leave her alone with Chase. Not when she didn't have a good reason for running off and ignoring him since yesterday morning. All over a crib. *Add in that secret you can't seem to share.* "Chase, I'm—"

"I had a break in the case."

A mixture of excitement and relief wove through her. He wasn't going to put her on the spot. She peered into the kitchen. They might have five minutes before dinner, maybe less. "Let's go outside."

"I'm ninety-five percent certain our culprit is Crissy."

"Really? What happened?"

"You happened." Chase dipped his gaze to her lips, then away at the tree line. It wasn't fair how badly she craved his kiss. "You recognized that lipstick case."

"You proved it was hers?"

"Well, not exactly. But she has another one just like it. Tell me how many women in this town special order three-hundred-dollar lipstick from France? It can't be many." He relayed the story of him literally bumping into her at the grocery store, her purse spilling on the sidewalk. "I can't use that as evidence, though."

"Guess not." She looked up at him. "So what *are* you going to do?"

Chase dug his fingers into the base of his neck. "I don't know, Laurel. Ryder thinks I've turned into a conspiracy theorist. Chief probably does too. Oddly enough, your brother is the only one who doesn't think I'm delusional."

"Cody?"

"Marc."

That *was* surprising.

"I'd really like to talk to Arnie Powers, but I think Ryder might arrest me as a public nuisance if I bother him."

"I don't understand why he's—" Mom's eardrum burst-inducing whistle echoed—the Evans' family dinner bell. It was the only truly loud noise that didn't set Melly to tears. In fact, the baby usually giggled in delight. "You know we have to go inside—"

"—right now."

"Everyone sit down," Mom announced as Laurel closed the sliding door behind her. "Where's your sister? The middle one."

Laurel held up her hands in surrender, still shocked that Sadie had made the trip for Melly turning one month. Cody was no doubt behind that miracle, though she hadn't been able to steal a moment alone with him to ask. She only hoped she didn't regret the favor, especially with Chase invited for dinner. Sadie was a wildcard. Anything was possible. "Don't ask me."

Mom leaned the upper half of her body down the basement steps and yelled, "Sadie Lynn Evans, if you're sleeping in this house tonight, you have thirty seconds to be seated at this dinner table, do you understand me?"

Most of the seats were already filled or spoken for. If Laurel wanted space from Chase, she'd have to subject him to Marc. She wouldn't do that to him when he already felt as though everyone else joining them for dinner was against him. He needed an ally, someone who believed in his instincts. Once this whole divorce business was behind them, maybe they could stay friends. The non-kissing kind would be safest, though not nearly as enjoyable. One glimpse at Cody, and she swore her brother was telepathically communicating with her.

These things don't just happen.

Mom huffed in defeat after Sadie didn't appear, taking her seat and saying grace. Laurel was secretly relieved her sister was absent. With any luck, she was already on the road back to Anchorage and forgot to mention it. The less drama at the dinner table tonight, the better.

Light conversation floated around the table, but Laurel sensed Marc and Dad's disdain for Chase's unexpected presence. Her family was fiercely protective of one another, and it was only now that she understood how they must've blamed Chase for her leaving. Probably thought he'd strayed. Guilt twisted tighter the longer the tension sizzled in the air. Secrets meant to protect the people she loved seemed to be doing just the opposite.

At least Haylee was being nice to her invited guest.

"You should bring Zeus by sometime to meet Melly. I want to get her used to dogs so I can get one down the road," Haylee said to Chase, ignoring the conflicting expressions from everyone else at the table.

"He's a licker," Chase replied with a light laugh, pretending to be unaffected by the judgment. Pretending because he was such a wonderful human being, despite the real emotions Laurel could sense. The anxiety and unease. Now that they'd shared a few kisses, she doubted that undeniable connection would simply sever after the ink dried on those papers.

I'll worry about that later.

"Sorry I'm late, everybody!" Sadie announced loudly. She didn't exhibit any sense of urgency by rushing to the table, but her presence as she casually made her way to the last remaining seat stole the room. It wasn't her striking red hair—the only Evans besides Grandma Kathy who was a redhead—or her bold wardrobe choice—a bright yellow midriff shirt and black leather pants—that oddly worked. It was her personality. The mix of audacious and crazy that left everyone holding their breath.

Except Mom. Sadie couldn't rattle her if she focused all her energy on the task.

"Sit," Mom barked. "You're *late*. Everyone else is nearly through dinner." The uncomfortable hush that fell over the table made Laurel want to grab her plate and sneak off to the basement. For weeks, family dinners had been minus Sadie—aka pleasant and mostly uneventful.

"Chase, what a pleasant surprise to see you here," Sadie said in that dangerously unpredictable tone that meant she might be sweet or secretly plotting an ambush. She scooted her chair in. "What's it been, five years?"

"Something like that." He forced a smile. Chase had never quite figured out how to take Sadie, but he never quitting trying. He had more patience than she did over the matter. Laurel loved him even more because of it. "Home for a visit?"

"Something like that," she repeated his words back to him as she cut into her pork chop. The gentle roar of side conversations started up again, and Laurel allowed herself to relax. Having Chase at the table wasn't so bad. In fact, it was kind of nice. *Don't get used to this*. Was that why Haylee was smiling so mischievously?

Laurel's relief was short-lived when Sadie blurted, "So I heard you and my sister are still hitched."

Silverware clattered against plates, Marc choked on his iced tea, and several sets of eyes stared both shocked and expectantly at Laurel and Chase. Though many had probably wondered *why* Chase was here, they certainly didn't seem prepared for that burst of news. Even Cody and Haylee appeared stunned into silence.

"This wasn't part of my plan," she heard Haylee whisper to Chase.

Laurel shot laser beams at Sadie, but her sister's smug expression didn't falter. *A warning?* "Do you enjoy leaving a path of destruction *everywhere* you go?"

"Girls, stop," Mom warned.

"It's true, isn't it?" Sadie pressed, ignoring Mom's reddening face. "Along with your pending job offer in the Florida Keys. Are you taking your *husband* with you this time or ditching him again?"

How Sadie knew wasn't Laurel's chief concern. It was Laurel's fault for not locking her bedroom door—something she never had to do when Sadie wasn't home. She set aside her irritation, focusing on the damage control.

"Enough!" Dad yelled, rattling even Sadie.

Through the tense silence, Laurel felt Chase's hurt gaze burn into her. She reached for his hand resting on his thigh, but he pulled it away when she tried to squeeze it. The rejection stung more than it should have. "Come with me," she pleaded to him quietly. "Please."

After several beats of reluctant silence, he nodded once. They carried their plates into the kitchen and slipped out the back door before the real tension took over the dinner table inside. Raised voices penetrated the enclosure of the house. Because half of her family could see them on the deck, she led Chase around the house to the driveway.

"I'm so sorry about that," Laurel said immediately. "I'm not taking the job offer. It's why I never said anything. I had no idea Sadie knew about any of that—"

"I can't do this."

Whatever apology Laurel had been in the middle of, she lost the words. Her chest squeezed painfully. "What are you saying?"

"I love you, Laurel."

Her hands trembled at her sides as she felt her world falling apart one shaky breath at a time. "There's a but in there."

"I can't do all these secrets. They're going to ruin everything good in your life." He paced in front of her briefly, ultimately heading down the driveway toward his truck. Halfway there, he stopped. "Sign the papers, Laurel. It's what you want to do, and I don't have the energy anymore to convince you to change your mind."

Chapter Thirteen

CHASE

"Don't look at me like that," Chase said to Zeus who was staring up at him from the foot of the bed, moping when he got out of the shower. For hours after Chase returned home from the disastrous Evans' family dinner the night before, the pup had paced, whined, and constantly stared out the window. Even though the dog couldn't tell him, Chase knew he was waiting for Laurel.

In only a few days, Zeus had bonded with her. *So easy to do.*

He didn't know how to make his dog understand

that Laurel had hurt him with all the secrets she'd kept. Not only from him, but her family. If she'd been open and honest from the beginning, Sadie wouldn't have been able to stir up a single ounce of drama. The frustration he'd been pushing down for days because of the ticking clock had all bubbled to the surface at once.

Time had run out for him.

Jenkins would open his doors within the hour, and that would be the end of it.

Another whine, and Chase's heart nearly cracked in two for the pup. "I'm sorry, okay?" He dropped onto the bed and wrapped his arms around the dog, hugging him close. "Sometimes things don't work out. I thought fate had other plans, but I was wrong."

Zeus licked his wrist.

"You'll still get to see her sometimes," he said, certain they'd run into each other at cookouts but not dwelling enough on that thought to upset him. She was a master at compartmentalizing her emotions; he could do it, too. "I'll take you fishing soon, with your *girlfriend*." Zeus' ears perked at the one word the smart pup had associated with Rowdy.

The clock on his dresser warned him he needed

to get a move on it. Today was all he had to figure out these fires before he had to submit the reports, or Bauer would take over and submit his own, likely never again fully trusting in Chase's abilities. "You have to stay here this morning," Chase told Zeus as he dug through his dresser for a pair of jeans without a tear in them.

He found a pair in the bottom drawer, banging his elbow on the dresser on the way up. The stack of books on the corner toppled to the floor, along with a pamphlet he didn't recognize. He considered leaving the mess for later, but the headline on the brochure made him do a double-take. *Adoption: Understanding Your Options in Alaska.*

"Another secret, Laurel?" he grumbled, remembering she'd been in his bedroom twice recently. Why she would hide this here was beyond him, but none of the reasons he could think of made him any less upset.

Zeus hopped off the bed, sniffing at the pile of books, then the brochure.

Collecting the fallen items, Chase couldn't help but wonder if their whole marriage had been built on secrets he still didn't know. What else hadn't she told him? The job offer in the Florida Keys had been shock enough. But *adoption*? He'd had enough of secrets to last him a lifetime. Maybe longer. *No time to dwell on this anymore. Too much at stake.*

"C'mon, Zeus. I'll get you a treat before I leave." That cheered the forlorn pup right up.

At the fire station, Chase lost himself to the case. The one he would have to solve all on his own before the clock struck five. He put his phone on silent, closed the office door, pulled out a neglected whiteboard from the closet, and set to the task of studying the photos, notes, and evidence from both scenes. It would be so much easier if he could question people without a barrel of grief from Ryder and Glenn. He scribbled his notes on the board, drawing lines to oddities that seemed to connect and starring questions he would risk via a couple of phone calls before the day was over.

"You hunting a serial killer?" Marc Evans entered the office, dressed in khaki pants and a dark blue polo with the vet clinic logo stitched above the breast pocket, and closed the door behind him. He looked too refreshed to be at the station for another therapeutic inventory.

Chase capped his marker and cautiously turned toward Marc. "I'd probably have more support if I was."

"Brought a peace offering." Marc held an energy drink out to Chase. "I remember you don't care for coffee."

"Thanks. But what's this for?"

"For one of my sisters trying to win an Oscar for most dramatic performance last night. For me being a jerk and treating you unfairly for years when I didn't have all the facts. Take your pick." Marc sat on the edge of Bauer's metal desk and folded his arms. "She hasn't signed the papers yet, but she's going to soon."

Chase's heart did a funny flip-flop at the news, which only irritated him. "I never meant to hurt her," he said to Marc. "I just—"

"I know." Marc stared off at the board for several seconds before he returned his gaze to Chase. "Look, I'm not here to tell you what to do about Laurel. You two have to figure that out on your own. You're both adults. But I do have something you need to hear. About your cases."

"What's that?" He welcomed the change of subject, but didn't dare get his hopes up. That's what had gotten him into this mess in the first place.

"Stopped by to check on Arnie Powers this morning. You know, being neighborly and all since he got burned trying to put out that fire. Brought him a bottle of wine. No one in the Evans household drinks white zinfandel, by the way." Marc crossed his legs at the ankles. "Arnie had some curious things to say about that garage fire."

"Did he?" Chase couldn't help it; his heart beater faster of its own accord. Could this be the break he desperately needed in these final hours? It felt too good to be true. *Too easy.*

"That kerosene heater of Henry's was an older model. One of those that sounds like a Cessna engine when it's running, according to Arnie. Says he can always tell when Henry's running it, because he can hear it from his kitchen with the window closed."

Chase thought he knew where Marc was headed with this, and tried not to let his disappointment show. "The burn marks were consistent with that heater being the origin of the fire." He'd examined everything dozens of times the night of the fire, just to be certain. "You saw the burn patterns yourself."

"It *did* cause the fire," Marc agreed, pushing off the desk and approaching the whiteboard with interest. "But Henry didn't use it, just like he said he didn't. Arnie was home all evening. Claims he didn't hear the heater fire up until well after eight. An hour after Henry showed him the spice rack he'd finished building."

"If Henry didn't use the heater, who did?"

"Arnie says he saw Crissy working in the garden shortly after it fired up, but she was nowhere to be found when he saw the black smoke above the garage. Need me to draw a dotted line with one of your markers?"

"Don't suppose Arnie put any of this in an official statement?"

Marc shook his head. "He said Ryder asked him to come down to the station tomorrow. Guess the chief had to make a day trip to Anchorage for something."

Chase cracked open the energy drink and took a long swig. He hoped Ryder was in Anchorage keeping his promise to get Chase that claim figure and not for some unrelated errand. He checked his phone for any missed calls or texts, but for once, there was nothing. Why Arnie couldn't simply give his statement to Murph or any of the other officers only reminded him that his best friend thought he was overboard obsessed with this case.

"Thanks, Marc. This helps in more ways than you know."

"Don't thank me. Laurel strong-armed me into stopping by Arnie's this morning. Fired off questions like she was that woman in *Murder She Wrote*. I think she's in the wrong career field." He headed for the door, stopping with his hand on the knob. "It's not too late." He left before Chase could ask him if he meant Laurel or the case.

Chapter Fourteen

LAUREL

Laurel sat on the edge of her bed, wedding ring cupped in her hand, and stared at the empty window. Was it strange that she wished Ed were peering in at her now? Hadn't that crazy moose been there for her best friends in their moments of need? "Where are you now, you big lug?"

Jenkins Law Office opened earlier that morning, but she hadn't traveled any farther than the two blocks to Arnie Powers' place and back. Turning down Marc's offer for a white chocolate mocha afterward, she'd sent her brother on his way with the information she hoped would help Chase with his investigation. It was the least she could do for him after all the harm keeping secrets had caused. No one could threaten her report or her job for being a concerned neighbor.

All week, she'd been dead set on signing the papers to take care of a *technicality*. But it was Chase's haunting words from last night that stuck with her now. *Sign the papers*. One signature and they could go their separate ways. Selfishly, she didn't want him to want that. Why hadn't she figured that out sooner?

"Stupid secrets," she muttered.

Unclasping her fist, she studied the gorgeous ring, unable to stop the flood of emotion from the memories it conjured. Chase wasn't known for big romantic gestures, but he'd certainly pulled one off that day. Popping the question at a cliffside point a few miles from town with a dramatic view of the sunset.

"One last time," she said to the ring, slipping it onto her finger. She held up her hand, admiring the way it looked, giving in to the memory of Chase almost dropping it over the side of the cliff when he tried to put it on her. They'd laughed all the way back down the trail, so happy and carefree. So in love. No idea that their lives would be torn apart hardly a year later.

Rapid knocking at the door caused her panic. She tugged at the ring. "Just a minute." The more desperate she grew to remove the ring, the more resistant it became. "You can't be stuck," she muttered. "Why are you stuck?"

"Laurel?"

Mom's voice sounded through the crack in the door half a second before she pushed it the rest of the way open. Laurel barely had time to fold her hands and hide the ring. "What's up?"

"Sadie left."

"I'm not going to say I'm sad about that." She'd been blaming her morning reclusiveness on avoiding her sister, waiting for her to get on the road back to Anchorage. It would be a while before she spoke to Sadie after the stunt she pulled last night. To rub salt into the wound, Sadie hadn't attempted an apology.

"You girls are going to have to work through your issues one of these days."

"Not today."

Mom let out a soft sigh and took a seat beside Laurel. "It's true, right? You're still married to Chase?"

With a deep breath, she relayed the same story to

Mom that she had with Marc earlier that morning. "I missed a signature, five years ago. Apparently, it wasn't caught until recently. I've only known for a week. Jenkins is back in his office today, and he has the papers. All I have to do is sign that one line I missed, and it will be officially over."

"Is that what you want?"

No. Laurel had never wanted the divorce. She thought she'd been doing Chase a favor. Thought he deserved someone better. He was right. Secrets were going to ruin everything good in her life. She'd come clean with both her brothers. *Mom's turn.* "I need to tell you the reason I left five years ago."

"I'm all ears, sweetie." Mom draped her arm around Laurel and listened to every word without an ounce of judgment. Unloading the truth felt wonderfully therapeutic. Despite the heavy nature of her story and the constant stream of soft tears, she felt lighter for sharing it.

"I can't have kids anymore." Laurel swiped at her soaked cheeks. "I've had too many doctors tell me the same thing to believe any differently." When she told her mom about the crib Chase made by hand, she started crying all over again.

"You don't have to sign," Haylee said, creeping into the room.

"You're a good eavesdropper," Laurel said with a laugh. "I thought you were completely against me moving out and abandoning you to the wolves." Mom snorted at that comment. "You were rather dramatic about it."

Haylee let out a sigh and plopped down on the bed beside Laurel, sandwiching her in. "You really didn't go back and read those texts from the other day, did you?"

"There were just so many."

Haylee bumped her playfully with her shoulder. "You don't have to sign those papers," she repeated, resting her head against Laurel's shoulder like she used to when she was seven.

"But I do."

Haylee grabbed her left hand, lifting it up in emphasis. "Then why are you wearing your wedding ring?"

"Stupid thing is stuck."

"How many signs do you need?"

Laurel looked up at the window, but Ed wasn't there. "Apparently one more."

"I'm sorry I pulled you both away from work," Laurel said to Ava and Kinley as they walked down the block toward Jenkins Law Office that afternoon. She'd used the group text from the other day to summon their support, bribing them with scones *and* coffee. She could handle the pesky signature on her own, but she wanted her best friends close by to help her through the aftermath.

She hated how final this all felt.

It wasn't fair to go through that painful feeling twice.

"We wouldn't let you do this alone." Kinley looped her arm through Laurel's as they strolled down the residential sidewalk, a block south of the main downtown strip. It was too pleasant a day to drive, but she didn't want to risk running into Chase by walking past the fire hall.

"I wish you weren't doing it at all," Ava admitted, looping her arm too. "But this is your life, not mine. We're here for you either way."

The day was too sunny and cheerful for what Laurel was about to do. It should be miserably over-cast with a downpour of rain. But even rain would be warmly welcomed in their current drought. *A bliz-zard would be oddly fitting.* She closed her eyes and sucked in a deep breath as they turned the last corner.

One step onto the street and Kinley jerked the trio to an abrupt halt. "Moose!"

Ed stood outside Jenkins Law Office, posted there like a guard who had every right to block the entrance. Laurel couldn't even bring herself to be surprised when the moose stared right at her. "You've got to be kidding me."

"Isn't that something," Ava said.

Laurel had to laugh so she didn't cry. "This is the same moose you all swear changed your love lives for the better?"

"Yeah. But today is your day. Want us to chase him off?" Kinley offered.

"No!" Laurel gripped Kinley's arm tighter to keep her from charging ahead. "I'm not letting my best friends get trampled by a disgruntled moose. For *any* reason." She stared back at Ed, wishing he could use words. But even if he could, would the moose tell her something insightful like *not* to sign the papers, or would he ask her for more of that sugary warm liquid he'd lapped up off the ground last week? Maybe he was a matchmaker, maybe he was a new coffee addict. Impossible to know for sure.

The women stood on the opposite sidewalk,

watching the moose as a truck drove between them. Ed didn't move a single hoof, but he sniffed at a decorative pot of forget-me-nots beside the entrance as if he had all day. The only way to the door was to go through him, and that wasn't an option.

These things don't just happen.

Laurel dropped her gaze to her wedding ring she hadn't been able to take off. "I ruined my second chance with him and didn't even know it," she said to her friends, glancing occasionally at the unmoving moose. "I took him for granted, and he won't forgive me this time. I have no one to blame but myself for how everything crashed and burned. That's why I have to sign now. He deserves to put this all behind him and move on."

"Or you could wait a day and trying *talking* to the man," Kinley suggested.

"I second Kinley's idea," Ava agreed.

Why is it so hard for me to spit out the truth to Chase? She'd been mulling that question around, mostly in the twilight hours when she was tending to Melly or tossing and turning in her bed. What was she really afraid of, especially now that she'd blown everything? "I don't want to disappoint him," she finally said to her friends.

"Tell Ed that," Kinley muttered.

"Better yet, tell *Chase* that," Ava said.

"He won't want to talk to me."

Kinley nudged her with her elbow until Laurel looked over and saw Chase rushing toward them. Her heart stopped in her chest, hoping and praying this was the happy ending she craved so desperately.

Chapter Fifteen

CHASE

Chase was about to holler at Laurel not to sign the papers when he spotted the moose blocking the door to Jenkins Law Office, seemingly without a care in the world as nearby tourists bravely—or stupidly, in his true opinion—raised their cell phone cameras. "Want to tell me this isn't fate?" he said to Laurel when he reached her.

"I haven't signed."

He let out a laugh. "I guessed that."

"We've got to get back to work," Kinley said, yanking Ava away with her. "We'll see you both for Taco Tuesday at Warren's tomorrow. Lots of wedding plans to go over! Laurel can fill you all in about the pink ties."

"Pink ties?"

"Her wedding, not mine," Ava said, stumbling over her feet before she allowed Kinley to lead her away. He gave her a nod that it was okay to leave them, then focused completely on Laurel.

"I can't have kids," Laurel blurted.

Holding up the brochure that had curiously ended up in his work binder, he said, "I guessed that. Why didn't you tell me?" He wanted to reach for her hand, but he was still hurt by her secrets and the decisions she'd made for them without consulting him.

"You can still have kids. It didn't seem fair to take that away from you. I tried to tell you so many times." She looked across the street as Ed sauntered toward a couple of foolish tourists who waited until the last possible second to get out of his way and avoid being charged. "You deserve someone who can give you what you want."

He pinned her with his gaze. "What I want is *you*."

"But Chase, I can't—"

"I'm hurt that you took away my choice. I wish you'd come to me. Been honest with me from day one and let me decide for myself. I can tell you with absolute certainty I would've picked you. What happened feels so unfair, but it happened to both of us. You're not alone in this. You've never been alone. It's *you* I want. We'll figure out the rest. But absolutely no more secrets and no leaving. Being married means we work through everything together."

She stared at the ground for a few beats, reaching her fingertips for his, then looked back up at him. "Okay. No more secrets."

"And no leaving. That part's equally important."

"I'm staying here, I promise."

He wanted to kiss her, but the startled screams across the street stopped him. Ed had turned back because the same pair who'd gotten too close to him the first time were set on pushing their luck again. "Are you kidding me?" he muttered.

"I think they have coffee," Laurel said in a near whisper.

"Get back!" Chase hollered at them, praying he wouldn't be calling the ambulance down the street.

A yelp of a siren echoed as the flashing lights of a patrol car crawled along the road. He expected to see Ryder behind the wheel, but it was another officer, Murph. "She can handle this," Chase said to Laurel, interlacing his fingers fully with hers. "I think we have a few things to talk about. Like when you're moving back in. But we need to grab Zeus or he won't forgive me. That poor sap has been miserable since you left us."

"I didn't—"

Chase cut her off with a kiss, right there on the corner of Mooseberry Lane and Forget-Me-Not Drive. It was the busiest intersection in town. All of Sunset Ridge would know they were back together by the end of the day, and he couldn't be happier about that.

After a few hoots and whistles, Chase let Laurel come up for air. Her eyes were a shade darker, her evident happiness dancing in them. "C'mon, we have to get Zeus."

Hand in hand, they strolled the three blocks to the fire hall where his truck was parked. "What ever happened with your case?"

"You mean since you and your brother turned into private investigators?"

"We were just being neighborly." Laurel's eyes twinkled with mischievous flirtation as they approached the fire hall. "By the way, no one in our house drinks white zinfandel."

"So I've heard." He helped her into the truck because he could, closing her door when she was comfortably seated. Once inside the cab, he added, "I submitted the report as inconclusive: possible arson."

"Possible?"

"I don't exactly have video footage or eyewitness accounts to the setting of either fire, and I have to wait on Ryder to get back from his Anchorage errand so Arnie can submit an official statement. But I have enough to provide reasonable doubt on either fire being an accident. Even came across some photos I took last summer of that *cabin* that prove it wasn't habitable. I don't think the insurance company will be too happy to see those." He turned down a residential street, headed for their house. He sure liked the sound of that. *Their house.* "Even still, it's not enough to call it arson outright, but it should be enough to keep that insurance claim from paying out. That's obviously her goal—to get the money."

"Crissy Davenport?"

"Yeah." He reached across the center console for her hand, loving how they were working so effortlessly as a team. For five years, his life had been empty. Even when he tried to move on to someone new it only confirmed that Laurel was it for him. Fate had known as much and given him a few helpful nudges this past week.

"You think Henry is oblivious to what she's up to?"

"Yeah, I do. I've looked him in the eye enough to believe he's as confused as everyone else."

"He's such a nice guy. How did he end up with —" Laurel gasped so loudly Chase slammed on his brakes a few feet short of the driveway. It took him half a second to follow Laurel's panicked gaze to the side of his house. Crissy Davenport held a square blue container he instantly recognized as kerosene.

Laurel shot out of the truck like a rocket while the truck was still in gear. "Get Zeus!"

Chapter Sixteen

LAUREL

Laurel raced across the yard toward Crissy, determined to reach her before she could ignite the dumped kerosene, and driven even more when sunlight gleamed off a silver lighter. No one was setting fire to their house without suffering a few broken bones. She prayed Chase listened to her to get Zeus out of the house, in case she wasn't quick enough to stop Crissy.

The flame flickered from the lighter, a crazed look in Crissy's eyes. Laurel had half a second to take in her ratty hair and disheveled appearance before she tackled her. Crissy cried out when her body slammed into the ground.

"This is all your fault! You and your stupid boyfriend," Crissy screeched.

"He's my *husband!*"

A string of obscenities followed from Crissy. Laurel was more focused on the lighter that flew out of Crissy's hands than what spewed out of her filthy mouth.

The grass ignited in an ugly *whoosh!*

Laurel scrambled to her feet, but Crissy pulled her down by the ankle. Pain sliced across her knee. "I knew you were in on this too!" Crissy yelled at her, unconcerned about witnesses. It made Laurel question whether the woman had the discretion to set the other fires.

The crazed woman pushed Laurel onto her back and pulled back her fist.

Laurel kicked her away before Crissy's swing connected with her jaw. The flames in the dry grass spread at an alarming rate, growing dangerously close to the kerosene-drenched siding of the house.

She stomped at the fire, the flames licking her toes through her sandals.

"Laurel, back up!" Chase hollered.

"Zeus?"

"He's safe." Chase unleashed a fire extinguisher on the grass, but that didn't stop Crissy from lunging at him. Laurel used her shoulder to throw the woman off course, knocking her back to the ground.

"Laurel!" The voice was vaguely familiar, but she didn't turn to see who was shouting her name. She planted her feet, preparing for another dive at Crissy if the woman was foolish enough to try something else. "Laurel, I got it from here."

"About time you showed up," Chase yelled at Ryder, extinguishing the last of the flames.

Laurel released a breath she hadn't realized she'd been holding since the moment she spotted Crissy dumping kerosene along the side of the house. "What were you thinking?" she shouted at Crissy. "Our *dog* was in there! What kind of person sets another person's house on fire with their dog inside?" She was screaming the words now, her body trembling at the thought of losing Zeus at the hands of the evil woman. She wanted to pull out her hair and pluck her eyes, but she wasn't going to stoop to Crissy's pathetic level.

Chase grabbed Laurel by the wrist, redirecting her attention as Ryder cuffed Crissy. "Laurel, it's okay. The fire is out."

"No, it's not okay!"

"Ryder's going to take it from here, okay?"

"Crissy Davenport, you have the right to remain silent." As Ryder rattled off her Miranda rights, Laurel let Chase draw her into his arms as her body trembled from the adrenaline rush. His embrace instantly soothed her frayed nerves. "W-we have to clean up that kerosene. It's so dry—"

"I'll handle it. Fire expert, remember?" He kissed the top of her head, holding her tighter. There was literally no better place she'd ever been than in his arms. How had she ever been foolish enough to walk away from this? *Never again.* "Let's go check on Zeus. He's in the truck and dying to see you."

With his arm protectively around her back, she walked with him, instantly feeling better at the sight of Zeus zooming around the cab of the truck. The closer they got, the louder he whined. That goofy dog was part of their family, and she'd missed him terribly these past few days.

"Told you, he was beside himself thinking you were never coming back."

Chase opened the door and Zeus rushed Laurel so fast they fell onto the grass together in a tumble. She held him tight against her as he licked both her cheeks. "I missed you too, buddy. Don't worry. I'm not going anywhere ever again."

Chapter Seventeen

Laurel

Laurel carried the second-to-last box from her car back into their house, so ready to be done with this moving business. The sooner she unpacked, the sooner they could truly enjoy their weekend as husband and wife. Now that the investigations were wrapped up, they could finally relax.

Crissy Davenport confessing to both arsons wasn't surprising, especially after learning that the combined total of the insurance claims added up to almost half a million dollars. That kind of money explained her crazed behavior. She confessed to her plot to skip town and leave her husband in a home.

Large sums could make people greedy and desperate enough to seek revenge on anyone standing in their way. When Chase submitted his report as a possible arson, Crissy retaliated.

Laurel had been with Chase when he told Chief Bauer about the claim amount and remembered how quickly the chief's face dropped in shock. The man wasn't likely to doubt Chase's instincts ever again. No one considered Crissy was seen by a dozen neighbors trying to burn down their house.

The most shocking twist was the insurance adjuster. Aside from the icky vibe the man exuded, Chase kept insisting it was odd for him to withhold the claim amount. But when Crissy threw Tuck Granger under the bus for his part in the fraudulent scheme, everything became much clearer. He was helping Crissy push the claim through, fully expecting a cut of the payout.

"That it?" Chase asked Laurel at the doorway, taking the box from her.

She'd accumulated more belongings than she realized while living with her parents these past six months. Adding in the boxes she'd been storing at Chase's and stupidly loaded into her car last week, all of it added up. It would take her days to unpack it all and put her things back where they belonged.

"One more."

He stole a quick kiss, as he had each time they'd met at the door, claiming they had quite a few kisses to make up with those five years spent apart. Laurel didn't argue with that logic. At this rate, her toes would be permanently curled in bliss.

"Hey, whatever happened to Henry?" Laurel asked, leaning against the door. "I know he didn't have anything to do with the arsons, but is he okay after finding out his wife wanted to skip town with all that money?"

"Ryder happened."

"What do you mean?"

"Ryder took him to Anchorage for an appointment. While Ryder went to the insurance office for answers, Henry went to see a specialist. He didn't want anyone to know—you can imagine why—and it's a good thing he didn't tell anyone. Doubt Crissy would've been on board with him going because he's perfectly healthy. Not a trace of dementia or Alzheimer's. Crissy admitted to hiding his keys in the freezer after she heard that. He's upset, of course. But he'll get through it."

"I'm glad he's okay."

"Thanks to your private investigator skills." He

leaned in for another kiss, this one tempting her to abandon the last box as she melted into him.

Life wasn't going to turn out exactly the way they had planned it, but they were ready to adjust course together. They were already discussing adoption options and scheduled to visit the adoption agency in a couple of weeks. For the first time, this direction felt *right*. They'd decided it together, and that changed everything for Laurel.

"Hurry up and grab that last box so we can start the movie," Chase said, breaking apart the mind-melting kiss. "Zeus is threatening to eat all the popcorn."

Laurel hurried back to her car, sporting a swoony smile. It was impossible not to be filled to the brim with hope and happiness. She was so distracted thinking about the many, many years ahead for her marriage that she didn't notice Ed until she closed the car door.

She squeaked and dropped the box. Thankfully, only clothes were inside it. He was enormous this close up.

The moose, standing little more than five feet from her car, tilted his head in her direction like a curious dog.

"I don't have any coffee in that box if that's what

you're wondering," she said with a laugh. Maybe she should be more afraid of his proximity, but he didn't appear to be a threat to her. He seemed to be looking for a handout. "Even if I *did* have a white chocolate mocha, there's no way that's good for your diet."

Ed snorted, as if in disdain.

"I've created a monster."

Zeus whined from the front door, drawing Ed's attention. The moose lifted his head and looked at the door.

"I know it's hard to believe, but he doesn't have coffee either."

Ed maneuvered his massive body until he pointed toward the street, and trotted down drive-way. He was heading in the right direction to pass Black Bear Coffee. Laurel chuckled, wondering who he might startle today. "I never said thank you," she called after him.

The moose didn't look back, but she smiled anyway.

Epilogue

CODY

Cody Evans was the last to arrive at his parents' thirty-fifth wedding anniversary party at the Sunset Ridge Lodge. It was the last full day of kayaking tours for the season, and it was a busy one. He'd scrubbed his hands three times but they still smelled like the bay, and sand was likely in his hair. But he was here. That was what was important.

The party room was packed with half the town, and it made him smile to witness the turnout. Jerry and Beth Evans were well-loved in the community and it showed. As much as he admired his parents for sticking it out this long together, Cody would never know what that felt like. The adventurous lifestyle he preferred made committed relationships hard, which was reason enough for him to avoid them.

A quick scan of the room and he locked gazes with Haylee holding a wide-eyed Melly. The baby lit up like a lightbulb at the sight of Cody. He'd never given much thought to what it'd feel like to be an uncle before meeting Melly for the first time four months ago. Now he couldn't wait to spoil his niece with treasures from his travels.

Weaving his way through the crowded room toward Haylee, Cody spotted a woman with jet-black hair sitting in a corner chair, head tucked into what he suspected was a book. *Odd.* He couldn't see her facial features to determine whether he knew her or not, but he thought he'd remember a woman who preferred reading a book to mingling during a noisy celebration.

"Thought you weren't going to make it," Haylee said, bumping him with her shoulder when he got close enough.

He laughed. "Yeah, right. I have to sleep in the same house you do. At least for a few more nights."

Melly kept staring at Cody, even after Haylee handed her over. Those big blue eyes were going to melt some serious hearts. *Probably break a few too.* Cody glanced at his youngest sister, reading more in her mostly blank expression than she probably cared to know.

"So, you're really going for three years this time?" Haylee asked with a slightly sad smile.

"That's the gig."

"Dad's okay with that?"

"We got it all worked out." Cody fished his phone out of his pocket, suspecting a view from the back porch of his soon-to-be Maui home would cheer her up. "Could you say no to this?" He turned the screen displaying an ocean sunset toward her. "I'll get to see that every night."

"I really hope that isn't some photo they stole off the internet to entice you to take the job. You might get there and find out you really only have a wonderful view of a fence or a brick wall." As pessimistic as she sounded, he caught the excitement dancing in her eyes.

"You can come visit anytime."

Haylee took Melly back into her arms. "That might not be on the agenda for a while." She ran her hand over Melly's forehead, planting a soft kiss there. "Melly'll be walking before you come home."

"Three years old, she better be running in the

Moose Days marathon."

"You're not going to get to meet your new nephew either." Haylee nodded at Laurel across the room. Chase held his arm protectively around her, as if he weren't about to let her get away again. They were days away from meeting a little seven-year-old boy they hoped to adopt before Christmas.

Cody felt truly happy for them both. Not only for the soon-to-be new edition to their family, but for having found their way back to each other. He always knew they would, he just never knew how it would happen. Fate was funny like that.

"I'll get to meet him when I get back." As cheerful as he tried to sound, he felt a slight sting of loss at everything he'd miss. The position, as many others he'd taken over the years, required he stay on the island unless there was an emergency. He'd never been gone more than seven or eight months at a time. Always home for the summer kayaking season. But the Maui gig was too good to pass up. It would open doors for some amazing opportunities in the future, but it required he commit to three full years.

An odd sensation tickled the back of Cody's neck, but when he reached back to rub it away, he found nothing. He turned discreetly to look behind where he'd been standing and found the black-haired woman staring right at him. He felt a tinge of familiarity, as if he'd seen her in a magazine once.

Because she didn't even offer a smile, he nodded.

She didn't look away, but he did when Haylee spoke again.

"You can't even come home for Christmas?" Haylee pleaded. "One or all of us might throw Sadie out an upstairs window without you around to stop us. Could you live with yourself if Melly's mama was serving time?"

Cody laughed unexpectedly, which caused Melly to giggle in delight. It drew his attention away from the woman for a few beats, and when he looked back toward the corner, she was gone. "You should try meeting her halfway," Cody suggested, discreetly scanning the room for the mysterious woman.

"You *are* talking about the same sister I am, right? Redhead. Fiery temper. Flair for the dramatics. Breathes fire."

"She's not *that* bad." Cody might be the only Evans sibling who truly understood Sadie, and he felt another ounce of guilt for abandoning her when she needed him most. Unlike the others though, she would likely take him up on his offer to visit—more than once. If he wasn't careful, Sadie might just show up with all her stuff in tow and declare she was moving in.

"She almost broke up Laurel and Chase. You remember that reality-TV-worthy family dinner, right?"

"Secrets almost broke them up," Cody said, staring at Haylee hard enough to make her uncomfortable. He didn't have to press any further to get his point across, but he wanted to know if Haylee had given more thought to what they talked about a few nights ago. But before he could ask, the black-haired woman was standing directly in front of him.

"Are you Cody Evans?" she asked.

Meeting her dark eyes, Cody felt an odd flutter in what he swore was his soul. He confirmed that he didn't know the woman, but she looked so vaguely familiar to him that he couldn't understand *why* he didn't recognize her.

"Yes, this is Cody," Haylee answered for him.

He was never one to be lost for words. He might take his time to contemplate an answer, but never did words escape him as they did now. He didn't care for it one bit. "And you are?"

"Jenna." She untucked the book from her grasp and pulled out an envelope from between its pages, handing it to him. "Jenna Kingsley."

Kingsley. He knew that name. He needed a few moments to search his memories for a clue. He'd met dozens of memorable people on his travels and in Alaska. People from all over the world with wildly interesting stories. "What's this?" he asked, taking the letter the second time she poked it into his chest.

"It's from my late grandfather, Eddie Kingsley."

The breath deflated from Cody's lungs at the name. He'd first met Eddie in Barbados, but mostly they spent time together right here in Sunset Ridge. Except, Eddie hadn't visited this past summer. "I'm sorry for your loss. I had no idea he passed."

"It was very unexpected." Jenna nodded at the letter, a stern expression etched into her face. "I was instructed to deliver that to you in person."

Because Cody didn't know what else to say to that and the shocking news still processing, he simply said, "Thank you."

Jenna folded her arms over her chest, book tucked protectively in her grip. He briefly wondered what she looked like when she smiled. He bet she was breathtaking. "Aren't you going to open it?"

"Not tonight," Cody said, tucking the letter into a cargo pocket.

"Why not?"

He studied her with curiosity, working to unravel

the secret behind her impatience. But Jenna wasn't as easy to read as most people he encountered. That unsettled him a bit. "Knowing Eddie, I'll need to be sitting down somewhere quiet when I read that."

Jenna huffed a quick laugh, the faintest trace of a smile tugging at her lips. He was right. She was breathtaking. "Fair point."

"I'm really sorry about your grandfather."

"Thank you." She unfolded her arms, fidgeting with the book. "Let me know when you've read it, okay? I'm staying here at the lodge for now, until I get my grandfather's cabin."

"The letter has something to do with that?"

"Yeah. The will is . . . odd."

"Sounds like Eddie." They shared a fleeting smile. Though Cody had a flight booked to Maui in only a few days, he didn't mind the idea of Jenna Kingsley staying in town or the prospect of having to see her at least one more time.

"I better go check on my dog and make sure he hasn't eaten the pillows," Jenna said, turning to leave without another word.

Cody watched her go, fully aware that Haylee had witnessed the whole exchange. He could practically feel her wheels turning in excitement. The problem was, his were too.

Sign up for Jacqueline Winter's newsletter to receive alerts about current projects and new releases!

http://eepurl.com/du18iz

Other Books by Jacqueline Winters

SWEET ROMANCE

Sunset Ridge Series
    1 - Moose Be Love
    2 - My Favorite Moosetake
    3 - Annoymoosely Yours
    4 - Love & Moosechief
    5 - Under the Mooseltoe
    6 - Moosely Over You
    7 - Absomoosely in Love
    8 - Perfectly Moosematched
    9 - Almoose Love
    10 - Chrismoose Kisses

Starlight Cowboys Series

1 - Cowboys & Starlight

2 - Cowboys & Firelight

3 - Cowboys & Sunrises

4 - Cowboys & Moonlight

5 - Cowboys & Mistletoe

6 - Cowboys & Shooting Stars

Christmas in Snowy Falls

1 - Pawsitively in Love Again at Christmas

2 - Pawsitively Home for Christmas

3 - Pawsitively Yours for Christmas

Stand-Alone

*Hooked on You

STEAMY ROMANTIC SUSPENSE

Willow Creek Series

1 - Sweetly Scandalous

2 - Secretly Scandalous

3 - Simply Scandalous

About the Author

Jacqueline Winters has been writing since she was nine years old when she'd sneak stacks of paper from her grandma's closet and fill them with adventure. She grew up in small-town Nebraska and spent a decade living in beautiful Alaska. She writes sweet contemporary romance and contemporary romantic suspense.

She's a sucker for happily ever after's, has a sweet tooth that can be sated with cupcakes, and is a dog mom to a lovable Alaskan Husky. On a relaxing evening, you can find her at her computer writing her next novel with her faithful dog poking his adorable nose over her keyboard, demanding treats and/or pets. Usually both.

Made in United States
Orlando, FL
12 July 2023

34960026R00139